SAPPHO'S
OVERHEAD PROJECTOR

Bonnie J. Morris

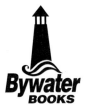

Bywater
BOOKS

Ann Arbor
2018

Bywater Books

Print ISBN: 978-1-61294-139-4

Bywater Books First Edition: November 2018

Printed in the United States of America on acid-free paper.

Cover designer: Ann McMan, TreeHouse Studio

Bywater Books
PO Box 3671
Ann Arbor MI 48106-3671
www.bywaterbooks.com

This novel is a work of fiction.

For these six particularly beloved bookworms:
Deb, Dix, Dorothy, Cindy B., Nev, and Susan

Introduction

*Sappho's Guest Lecture
and the Overhead, Herself*

Hannah left the meeting in the Dean's eighth-floor suite determined not to cry. No, she wouldn't give him the satisfaction. Her face stonily composed, she walked to her office and began to yank pushpins out of the walls, sending her framed art posters crashing onto the worn industrial carpet.

No tenure for Dr. Stern. Her position was going to be *terminated.*

The entire history program had, apparently, been targeted for "strategic downsizing." Just two tenured professors (both male) would remain, folded into a hallway behind the study-abroad unit. Women's history would be eliminated as a major—"It has been a bold experiment here," the Dean had purred. And Hannah's former office? Her beloved townhouse building was going to be turned into a new subway stop.

Goodbye, and good luck. Hope you find work somewhere else, dear.

❧ ❧ ❧

5

At six p.m., worn out from a lonely day of packing up her office, Hannah sank back into the bathtub, adding Lux until a foam of argan-scented bubbles covered her breasts. But no fragrant oil could soothe her skin; no alcohol in the house came close to numbing her panic. She'd have to go over to Sappho's Bar and Grill later on—let Isabel, who was now her lover as well as the bar owner and bartending mystic, make her a potion. Food, though, seemed to whet her appetite for rage and revenge. Chipotle chocolates in particular. She nibbled one now, smashing another with wet fingers and smearing it into a bronze-hued women's symbol on the tile wall. Then she shut her eyes and visualized, again, the line of subway representatives who had swarmed so importantly through her office the other day. Plucking blueprints from crisp folios, they had measured her office shelves and walls for imminent destruction even as she sat there tapping final grades into her computer with all the concentration she could summon. Erasure. Erasure of her time there, twenty years of grading in that space. Even her office phone was to be disconnected. How would her former students contact her? Her scholarly colleagues, her archival pals? Would that beloved familiar extension number ring and ring, fated to become a passive subterranean echo? Where did missed connections go, in the end—a parking lot in hell, an eternally flowing stream of canceled conversations?

She watched her bathtub water, like her teaching career, going down the drain.

The next day, as Hannah grimly piled her art and syllabi into old watermelon crates and boxed up textbooks she'd taught for years, she worried that she might leave something valuable behind by accident.

Could a class outline get stuck on a nail, in a crack in the wall, or slide under the old tacked rug? And if so, when the snug egg of her old existence cracked under phallic drill bits of subway renovation, would the underground workers far below find evidence of her teaching life, trickling down like cave moisture? Jutting out of the underground walls like jagged gems of feminism in a diamond mine? Would fragments of her old class notes be discovered, years or centuries later, lost bits and pieces preserved and entombed like those amber-trapped insect bodies in the *Jurassic Park* movie, holding within them the DNA of women's studies as it was once taught? Would her lesson plans be *discovered* one day like the Dead Sea Scrolls, like Sappho's poetry, like cave art on a Neolithic wall, as the Venus of Willendorf statue herself had been found? Only this time it would be not archaeologists but subway workmen in scratched hardhats, marching through a dirty tunnel space with pickaxes under their arms like the Seven Dwarves?

And then the lightbulb came on full beam above her head.

What if all that Neolithic art, those goddess statues, the evidence of women's sacred feminine past that male explorers found in caves, was just the teaching material left behind by some even more ancient women's studies professor? Someone whose office . . . UP THERE . . . was shut down, taken apart before her work was complete? Like me?

What if the art slides Hannah used in her class lectures on women's heritage were actually images of goddess figurine toys that had slipped off the desk of some earlier, earliest grand lecturer, an overhead professor as uprooted and bereft as Hannah felt now, but uprooted from where? From *UP THERE?*

All right. Who was the giant professor up above,

the lesson planner in the heavens, the great Overhead women's history department chair who had lost her place and who now floated in space? How could Hannah . . . and maybe Isabel, too . . . find her, and restore that lost department in the sky, and even join it as a lecturer again?

Would she have to be . . . dead?

On Tuesday, having surrendered her university ID and office keys, Hannah walked disconsolately into Lecture Hall B-12 for a final nostalgic visit. Here, she had made the past visible, selecting what she believed students must know about women's differing histories. She gave a loving pat to the wobbly overhead projector, now shoved into a corner, its long electric cord wrapped like a protective dragon's tail around an aging, soon-obsolete body. This had been her old standby when DVD films failed to load, just images laid over a light box, projected against the two big screens. Sappho, Queen Liliuokalani, Bessie Jackson. How it made them real, huge, larger than life, undeniable!

She was alone. She was on her way to nowhere, fired at middle age. This lecture hall had been her kingdom, or queendom, or playing field. Dr. Hannah Stern in the house; start note-taking! She closed her eyes, recalling that exhilarating moment at the start of fall term, when every student flipped a notebook open and began taking notes. Then it had changed from paper pads to laptops, but still, the pipeline had been assured: *Take note. Listen up. Carefully. This is what you need to know, the wisdom handed down. The passing of the torch, the water in the pipeline, women's mysteries. And will you catch that spark? And will you wade into those waters?* Some took it seriously and became torchbearers in feminism, and others were simply hoping for an easy A and challenged their B+. Well, who would come in and stop her if she taught one last lecture now?

In her pocket was a brochure for the Mediterranean goddess cruise she'd planned to take . . . before losing her job and needing a whole new budget. No Olivia cruise this summer. No fun ever again. But she could dream for free. She slid the brochure onto the surface of the projector. She'd project images of happy lesbians, partying on a ship's deck, as her last stand. Her *bon voyage*.

But before she could bend to turn on the overhead projector, both of the dual wall screens lit up. The projector whirred to life. Sappho's face rose up on the huge light panels, watchful, fierce, benevolent.

Hannah jumped back, stupefied: *But I didn't plug anything in yet. In fact, I couldn't have turned it on. My passcode was just canceled. I no longer have my university ID!*

Then the lecture hall filled up with every student she had ever taught, two or three to a seat, holding in their laps spiral notebooks, sketchpads, computers, day planners. Every pen and finger was raised to start note-taking.

"Walk right in," boomed Sappho's voice, undulating from the overhead projector. "And sit tight, now. All of you. Listen to me, sisters. We're going for a ride."

Sappho's guest lecture might have lasted a year, or longer. Hannah couldn't tell. She and all her former students were under the spell of the lyre, and swept up in the great recital of ancient women's knowledge that had never been written down. Always, it had been passed along orally, until a few, like Sappho, dared to write down poems of women's love, only to have such words burned. Now the overhead projector of Hannah's old lecture hall showed the course of goddess history, the span of earthly time from a woman-centered belief system and life cycle to the coming warfare of patriarchy. Here were the goddesses of mercy and compassion ranging from ancient Babylon to China, from Iceland to Guatemala; the great Egyptian pharaoh Hatshepsut, the Dianic and Mycenaean cultures, vestal virgins dancing in the sisterhood of guarding women's temples. Diana. Gaia. Aphrodite. The Nordic goddess Freyja, Ragana of Latvia, Spider Woman of the Navajo, Lakshmi and Durga and Kali, Pele and Oya and Anansi and Hine and Kunapipi.

Then the class saw all the women whose folk rituals were abruptly declared witchcraft, their torture and martyrdom assured. Now terrified women turned on their own, naming old friends as witches and blasphemers; here were the queens like Spain's Isabella who found power in piety, ordering the Inquisition to burn other women alive. Other queens were once girls, married young to ambitious older men, locked away in towers; other girls were raped by wandering men and came to beg for mercy from these queens, their illegitimate pregnancies a mark of village shame. *For Mary Hamilton's borne a babe.* Songs passed warnings to women, between women, and many a song and lullaby held hints of the old Goddess. But men had the law on their side. Always.

Then Sappho seemed to find a place of pause, intoning, "Class dismissed." The students of Hannah's long classroom career rose and bowed, saluting both Hannah and Sappho with their spiral notepads and sheathed laptops raised in tribute, and they vanished, leaving chalk dust. Sappho stepped forward from the flat two-dimensional plane of the projection screen, shook her gown once, and freed two enormous wings from shoulder blades that seemed to stretch forever, gathering Hannah in. The screen went blank. The room went dark. Beneath Sappho's wings, which enclosed and lifted her protectively, Hannah felt herself rising, until the chalk dust and splintered podium of her old classroom were below her.

Below her, beneath her. "That job was indeed beneath you," boomed Sappho, soaring toward some unimaginable upward rest stop, her gown never once flapping as the atmosphere heated and froze, pulsed with mist and baked with desert winds, ingathering time and space. "You're ready to do more. And we have work for you."

They rose above the familiar and unfamiliar, passing town water towers and radio broadcasting towers, the distant blinking signals Hannah had looked to from her window on so many nights, first while writing her dissertation and later during the long breakup with her lover before Isabel. Up past the towers, past tall buildings designating cities she had known, lived in, visited. Over the surf of oceans Hannah had known, and then above the shapes of hugely spouting whales. Then up above the footpaths of mountains Hannah once hiked on family vacations, over their snow-jagged crests and dry volcanic calderas, to the rims of other earthly peaks and constructions: Alps and pyramids, Himalayas and Mayan temples. Of a sudden they were hailed, midair, by a very old and steadily buzzing aeroplane. Hannah gasped as she recognized Amelia Earhart, who nodded and waved at her with one leather-gloved hand. "It's her! So, she's—"

"Orbiting," Sappho called over the world's broadest shoulder. "Orbiting and watching over us. Like so many misunderstood women, she just didn't want to be tied down."

11

They zoomed into darkness, around a bulky space station, and beyond. *"UP!"* shouted Sappho, and dense whirling clouds parted, finally revealing a floating slice of recognizable working women's space. It was Hannah's office. But not Hannah at that desk. A far grander figure, professorial mortarboard tilted on a massive head from which white hair flowed like water, rose to greet them, and Sappho deposited Hannah in the scarred red chair beside the desk—the chair Hannah once used for her own students during office hours. It still held the anxious sweat of every undergraduate who had ever come in to argue about a grade, to beg for an extension on an overdue paper, or, more thrillingly, to seize academia's greatest dare and declare a major in women's history. Hannah felt the chair alive beneath her legs, pulsing into her back. *"We've got your back, Dr. Stern,"* whispered the thousands of students she had taught. (Even those, Hannah marveled, whom she'd disappointed by explaining that, no, they wouldn't be earning an A; learn to live with the B+.) But why was she here? Why had she been summoned to office hours with, with . . .

For this was *She.* The great Professor-in-the-Sky, the Overhead, the Overhead Projector herself. The grand displaced department chair who orbited, like Amelia, in search of ways to restore women's history from its shattered vessels to its source. This was *She,* the Matriarch, the Goddess, who had lost her job to patriarchy, to God the Father. In that far more important and longer-unresolved tension than Hannah's own academic turnover, this was the wise one who had been told a better system was in place, a new telling of origins, a better explanation of Creation. And for how long had *She* floated, out of office, her calendar of rituals forbidden, her followers declared insane, heretical, banned and burned and pilloried and outcast? With rage, *She* drummed long fingers on Her desk, swept papers and clay figurines off its top where down to earth they fell, long buried, marveled at when found. And all her powers locked in that Projector, which sometimes hummed to life and turned on without warning, projecting truth and justice, downward-beaming. For the many feminists who had returned to Her, how harsh that office hours were near impossible to get. And classes canceled, but for times like these, when portals opened for the lost—like Hannah.

"Call me Ova," said *She*, anticipating Hannah's question. "It's short for Overhead, as you see. And Sappho is just one of my angels in waiting, as is Amelia, who finally found the flight she wanted, orbiting earth in protection of women, in service to me." She poured a jewel-like coffee brew from what had once been Hannah's old Thermos bottle, serving them both in Hannah's souvenir music festival mugs. Sappho, standing guard in her worn sandals, said "No thanks" in lilting Greek: *Oxi efcharisto.*

And the interview began. For, of course, this was what it was, the next and ultimate job interview for Hannah, with the goddess CEO, the Dean of Deans, the Big Document. Hannah dared one burning sip of Ova's coffee; instantly, she could hear the rhetoric of feminism pounding in her ears.

So you lost your job due to budget cuts. Because women's history isn't valued, yes. But, dear one: that is a very old story; they pushed me out from My job, too; and surely you can see you are not the first to be unjustly fired. Most women never gain the opportunities you've had. Let's look.

The overhead projector whirred again, showing

Hannah other scenes from history, anguished women's faces, shortened lives.

Here are the ones before you who lost their teaching jobs for being gay, in every university that feared a lesbian's power—refusing her right to be there.

Here are the ones never hired at all, before women's history was a subject taught in schools, whose knowledge was denied, belittled, lost.

She saw sociologist Pauline Bart, shamed and scolded by a skeptical male colleague who declared there wasn't enough material to teach one course on women's history; she saw Bart and feminist friends return in the night to tack up a list of one thousand women's names to that professor's door.

Here are the ones who never earned a graduate degree because they were not white, all doctoral programs closed to them in segregation's time.

Here are the ones who had an education through college, but never heard a word about women's history, only the ideas and accomplishments of men.

Here are the ones who never had an education, denied them due to gender, race, religion, disability or class—the girls burning to learn who learned in secret.

Here are the ones who made *women's history but who were thrust out of their new empowered roles when history changed: the Rosie the Riveter workers; the guardians of museums during war or those who hid treasures from invaders, but received no credit later; the All-American Girls Professional Baseball League; those who broke records of production and athleticism, written out of textbooks, names unknown.*

Here are the ones at the gates of higher education, qualified beyond the males admitted, forced into a quota system, not allowed to study "manly" subjects.

Here are the ones destroyed at birth because they were born girls.

Here are the ones allowed to live, but starved and stunted, married off at ten.

Here are the ones who worked as slaves when the law said one could not teach a slave to read.

Here are the ones beaten by their husbands for teaching slaves to read.

Here are the ones who taught themselves to read but never owned a book.

Here are the ones who walked ten miles to borrow books only to be told by so-called educated women, "This is a white library, honey—you can't come in."

Here are the ones who lost their jobs because they offered books and space to children who were not white.

Here are the ones who lost their jobs because they put books about being gay into the hands of gay kids.

Here are the ones who lost their jobs because they wrote those books.

Here are the one who lost their jobs because they sold those books.

Here are the ones who lost their jobs because they taught that those books existed.

Here are the ones whose contributions are being erased as history moves "online."

With each recitation, Hannah saw the eons during which women were denied their place in education, faces blinking as the great Overhead projected their stories, their histories. And as *She* pronounced each slight against the women across time, the Overhead swept an object off Her desk, figurines of women's history falling downward, coming to rest, Hannah understood, in caves and crevices on Earth, later to be discovered and misunderstood by men. What stayed with Hannah was that image of the little girl who had walked so many miles in her best clothes, her Sunday shoes pinching already blistered heels, awaiting the reward of just one book, only to be told that the free

15

public library books were in fact only for white children. There could be no going back in time to fix that record, to alter segregation and Jim Crow. There was, though, the writing that came from it, memoirs that told the story of suppression and survival. Those books held truths Hannah had assigned her own students to read. But now she had no students to mentor in that way.

"And what kind of position are you looking for now?" asked the Overhead, reviewing Hannah's curriculum vitae. Hannah reflected, *If She really is the great women's studies department head in the sky, this is the moment to ask for anything I want. Tenure at Yale, program director at Binghamton, guest lecture year at Oxford, research assistant to Alison Bechdel. But I think there's something more important to do. I think this isn't about me.* What she wanted, Hannah realized, was to get a bunch of books into the hands of that little girl once denied entry to the white library. Likewise, she wanted to put gay-positive books into the hands of kids living where homosexuality was still a crime. There was a mission for her—Sappho had said so— and it had something to do with circulating books, rescuing books. "Might I become some sort of radical librarian?" she ventured.

"You have chosen wisely," said *She*, "and named a sisterhood long devoted to my service, protecting women's knowledge from destruction and amnesia. This is the hour for all librarians and archivists to rise up in their place of work, and guard what has been so misunderstood: that women had a herstory, and like so many sea mammals that barely break the surface to be seen, the mere visibility is alarming and a target, though so much more is underneath. And, my dear, you understand this isn't an intervention of just one for one. This is a complete projection, a sliding of the right over the wrong, an overhead projection over time. It won't be easy. Think clearly of a place where you might work."

Where the books are. Where the history is. There's an office for me somewhere that sits exactly on the boundary between a trove of women's learning and all the lawmakers who ever denied access to learning based on race and sex. I want to occupy that office and defend the archived books. Where is that front office where those who would ban books by lesbians come face to face with those, like me, who dare to teach such books? Where are uptight Congressmen forced to take orders from gay librarians? In just one place, in America. One institution. And I know its name.

"I'll take one year at the Library of Congress," said Hannah, "to liberate women's history from the inside out. I've had this feeling, just a feeling, that something's being held there—a book that rightfully belongs to a girl, or girls. Maybe I can find and free that book. *Project* it somewhere, as I'm starting to understand. And—you can help me get that job?"

"Oh, yes; consider it done," said *She.*

And Sappho spread her wings.

Chapter One

Very Long Distance

Later that summer, in the sticky heat of August, Dr. Hannah Stern found herself at home in a place that wasn't home. She'd always felt focused and cozy in a library, any library, though she understood anew the privilege behind that sense of comfort and belonging. And this was *the* Library, the Library of Congress, which had granted her a one-year archival position. She now lived a good three states away from her lover Isabel—far away, too, from their beloved community institution, Sappho's Bar and Grill. But even if she had to spend this year alone, using her nights to apply for other jobs in academia, Hannah loved Washington.

The city bristled with diplomats, embassies, international cuisine, intrigue, bookstores. On her daily subway ride up to the Capitol South stop, she overheard arguments in French, Russian, Korean, Arabic, Hebrew, Farsi and Vietnamese. These were the languages, she realized, of America's wars; she was deep in the belly of policy and invasion, Pentagon and peace action. Someone had told her that the recorded announcement "Step back, please: doors

19

closing!" was a lesbian's voice, chosen out of all others during a Metro audition. Ordered by a lesbian to stay safe on her morning commute, and then at work handed armloads of rare manuscripts to catalogue, Hannah felt contentment lodge beneath her breastbone, the anger at having been pushed out of academia gradually being replaced by a better range of emotions.

The gay writer Alan Gurganus had once said, "Anger is a kind of B-emotion. Rage is as clear as gin." When even sorting out her feelings reminded her of grading former students, Hannah remembered that she was here to be useful, having enlisted in the alternative Secret Service of the Overhead Herself.

She'd packed only what she needed for a year of work, clothes and kitchenwares and some of her treasured books. The going-away party at Sappho's Bar and Grill had been an emotional feast, rather than a lamentation: Isabel, her partner, bar owner/host and practitioner of so many mysterious arts, had invited all their friends to a literary-themed dance with aphrodisiac drinks. Everyone Hannah cared about showed up with a book and a bouquet, and they dined on egg creams (the favorite treat in *Harriet the Spy*) and tarts shaped like Egyptian papyrus, each inscribed with a good-luck wish in lavender icing. "Now go read," shouted Letty, the bar's longest-but-not-oldest member, and quieter elder Trale added, "Be as selfish as you want. That means keep doing the work to get us on those shelves."

Get us on those shelves. When Hannah finally kissed Isabel goodbye at the airport, long, good kissing in that remote women's bathroom no one ever used, their noses and lips bruised from passion, Trale's words suddenly pressed on their atmosphere like a waffle iron. Hannah touched Isabel's soft brows. "Do you think books about us—about lesbian lives—are going to be lost again, or banned again, and rediscovered again decades later, in some sort of endless cycle?"

Isabel tucked in her blouse. "Endless cycles being my specialty, you know my answer. Yes. But I also think we took for granted that our history began to matter, and we really believed that women's bookstores would carry our stories forward longer than our own time."

And Hannah knew what she meant. They'd met in graduate school, Hannah completing her doctorate in women's history and Isabel dropping out to buy and remodel the local dyke bar. Isabel had furnished that beloved community space with rare books from women's bookstores around the world, at a time when those spaces and sites proliferated in every city and so many countries: from Amazon Books in Minneapolis to the Streelekha in Bangalore, India.

That collecting and shelving of the lesbian novels and herstories helped make Sappho's as much a space to curl up with a book as an active nightclub. The best local minds and quite a few aspiring writers had drifted into membership at the bar, finding in the unusual cocktails a quality of time travel no one could explain. On open mic nights, or during the events when the bar hosted readings by visiting authors, the vibe at the bar surged wavelike toward group recognition of the past.

And in all their herstories, differences were sharp and painful, yet there was, in that space, an overriding sameness in their lives as women who partnered with women, so that books or stories referencing lesbian survival drew cheers of recognition. When the poet at the mic or the song on the stereo referenced Paris in the interwar years, suddenly everyone was able to speak French; and if the lights changed or the food steamed with an aspect particular to another decade, well, weren't they all there to celebrate collective survival in its timelessness?

In silent agreement they all suspended doubt, embraced Isabel's magic as hostess and brewmistress. *What is she putting in those drinks? I'll have another. Did everyone see what just happened, or was it only meant for me?* Watching her lover serve women's history in each crafted martini, understanding that the past could be *consumed* and thus reenergize women of the present day—all of that had helped stir Hannah to preserve their literary trail. She manifested the scholarly inspiration that was just one intended result of Isabel's mixology.

Isabel, for her part, wasn't talking. Over the past year she had lifted the veil of ordinary time and shown Hannah glimpses of the women's history past, a year of frequent ghostly encounters Hannah would never forget. Now they were lovers, and in the future would be sharing a home—a cohabitation Hannah had to set aside for now. But, as she had stepped toward the security line and mouthed *I love you* to Isabel, she reflected that if academia had *pushed* her out, the Overhead had *pulled* her to this gig. She had a job to do, rescuing lesbian books—from what? For whom? Trale's words, again, tugged at her, "Get us on those shelves." Could she? Would she?

Isabel, watching Hannah walk away, mouthed silently the words, *So mote it be.*

Now Hannah had taken a one-year lease on a rented apartment near Dupont Circle, once the hub of D.C. gay and lesbian life, now coolly gentrifying to brand-name shops and chain eateries. It was the old neighborhood of Lambda Rising Bookstore and Lammas Women's Books, both institutions now gone yet well-remembered by the locals, who were happy to grant interviews about the heyday of LGBT bookshop readings and salons. Women's history might be poorly represented in the U.S. capital city's monuments and official guidebooks, but her own new neighborhood was alive with upstart commemoration: a Joan of Arc statue, an Underground Railroad marker, and was that Olivia Records' cofounder Judy Dlugacz she glimpsed, dining in the window of the French bistro? An avowed feminist congresswoman she recognized on sight coming out of a hipster eyeglass frame store, the top female sportswriter in the country coming into the bakery, and editors of local and national LGBT newspapers drank noisily together at the Malaysian restaurant that doubled as a gay bar.

She would always wrestle with this, her deep affection for radical celebrity, for the movers and shakers who made their mark in advancing women's progress. These were the figures in her own time who later would be, should be recalled as historically significant. But the famous were not the only ones who *made* history, Hannah reminded herself as she collected her book bag, ID badge and *Washington Post* and headed for the exit at Capitol South. This had always been her folly, to lecture on the public figures of the political past, without granting equal time to everyday women (and men) who had lived through the conditions of an oppressive past with dignity and with inventive means of survival.

The Madison Building connected to the Jefferson Building through a series of underground tunnels. It might be summer heat or winter ice outside, but at the LOC the climate was old paper, rare books

23

bulging, federal librarians rushing from appointment to appointment. School parties lined up at one door while smug scholars, ID cards flashing, used the "researchers" entrance. Amish visitors stood in reverent awe before one of the world's oldest Bibles while feminist detectives combed through the early papers of cross-dressing rebels. In one of the secretly located doughnut cafes, three young women fresh out of library school were plotting an exhibit on eighteenth-century cookbooks, blissfully unaware of the ironic contrast between their fast food snacks and their subject matter; men moving fragile boxes of materials between loading docks hailed each other with news and gossip about the latest Senate scandal.

Her job involved cataloguing recently donated women's collections by theme. More and more women who had participated in the whirlwind of second-wave feminism were now aging into their seventies and eighties, mindful of the need to downsize possessions and perhaps leave the good stuff to an archive or two. Those who had saved everything—treasured and tattered copies of *Sisterhood Is Powerful, Rubyfruit Jungle, The Wanderground, Loving Her,* even Tee Corinne's *Cunt Coloring Book*—were surely an annoyance to lovers and landlords as they moved boxes of yellowing literary ephemera from closet to closet over the years. But it was precisely because they had lived their lives *out* of the closet that made their holdings dear to them and dear to historians like Hannah, and her new coworkers at the LOC.

Now such women gladly signed over artwork, songsheets, broadsides and paperbacks that bellowed of feminist change and culture, proof of the network of independent women's presses that had flourished through the 1970s: Daughters, Diana, New Victoria, Shameless Hussy. And the names of the radical feminist newspapers, the likes of which had once flowed from every American state and nearly every large city, too! *Big Mama Rag. off our backs. The Lesbian Tide. No More Fun and Games. Hera.* Then there were the tiny pamphlets, and their larger single-sheet cousins, the broadsides, the poster art, the whole range of calls to action and calls to thought that had signaled awakening, awakening of the soul—in that time before social media and Facebook.

Putting such donor treasure troves in order was a daunting task. The regular staff was overwhelmed with special projects in addition to the usual exhibits, the presidential exhibits, the exhibits rushed onto the crowded fall calendar to accommodate unique papers on tour or on loan from abroad. There was always something on printmaking or publishing itself. Everything stopped when a fundraiser turned entire wings into private reception areas, or when a high-profile guest with a security detachment, often a Middle East dignitary, decided to stop by. Hannah was basically pinch-hitting for the real staff, who had of late been distracted in a hundred directions while the donations piled up. Every day, she arrived eager to see what The Pile would yield—she had quickly nicknamed the stack of file folders on her corner desk The Pile. Indeed, her immediate supervisor, a tough but tender-faced curator named Aurora, often greeted her with the interrogation, "So, Stern—how's The Pile coming along?"

Separate the latest donations from the earliest. Keep the dates of the contents on a different list from the dates of the donations. Divide into themes: politics, consciousness-raising, anti-racism, child-care and day-care activism, lesbian rights, wages for housework, The Equal Rights Amendment, the Equal Pay Act. There were membership lists and papers from organ-

25

izations: National Women's Studies Association, National Women's Political Caucus, the Feminist Writers' Guild, Daughters of Bilitis. Hannah had, at one point or another over her life, belonged to each of these. Then there were the women's music festivals, fifty or more, that had bloomed where planted in almost every state, including Alaska and Hawaii. Those programs and flyers, and the women's music concerts and artists touring year-round, formed another archive that could be an exhibit of its own— or directed into the Performing Arts Reading Room—or did it go to the LGBT collection? Who was she to decide? But this was her job. This was what she had asked to do, to be useful in the ways she had been trained . . . the ways her university no longer cared to pay her to do . . .

Don't think about that. Don't think about that. Think about the lesbian kid whose life will be changed if we get any of this material out there on exhibit. This is about visibility. The pipeline. The great torch-passing of culture from one tired generation to the next and youthful one. See what we did. See how we lived. Never forget. And she'd carefully turn to the next donation file, scanning the listed items for something really unique and thrilling, though all of it excited her: a signed copy of Simone de Beauvoir's *The Second Sex,* or that feminist carpentry memoir *Against the Grain.*

Gradually, Hannah came to learn the names of departments and elevator levels, the most interesting underground shortcuts, the best deals in the mouth-watering souvenir bookshop, which section heads should be avoided or sweet-talked as necessary, and when to sneak over to the Performing Arts Reading Room and listen to the rare and classic women's music albums donated by collectors and benefactors across time. It was a digital age, here in Hannah's late forties, yet vinyl and paper still dominated this snug world of preservation. After all, the focus here was history.

She'd noticed other funny anachronisms, too. The public telephone jutting out from the wall in the women's bathroom was a chrome inelegance she couldn't understand. Each time Hannah entered the stylish lounge, designed in some far earlier, leisured time, she was struck by the contrast between the smoothly tiled sinks, the spacious mirrors and private stalls, and the rusting pay phone that greeted visitors just before they entered the bathroom facility itself. Why, wondered Hannah, would someone stick a pay phone here? Never mind that they were now properly in the age of cell phones, debit cards, laptops, and email, with almost no one carrying change for a public phone or the necessity to use one at all for business calls. And who would conduct "business" in the middle of taking care of other urgent business? It always made her laugh and shake her head, as each day she nodded familiarly at the silent phone when entering the lounge.

But this was Washington, D.C. The Watergate scandal, Deep Throat in a parking garage, spies from other nations leaving clues and documents under park benches, under mailboxes, in shuffled papers, so perhaps some touring spy once used this "safe phone" to indicate a safe house, or call in an untraceable code-breaking message. One day Hannah noted the number on the bathroom phone: 202-554-4876. It didn't cue a memory of any famous spy film she had seen. Probably just a courtesy installation in the last era before cell phones, so that women could call anxious partners, bosses, school heads while on mini-break from touring Capitol Hill: "We're almost through here, then we go see the Supreme Court tour—meet you at five." Or: "One of the schoolkids

27

threw up at lunch time, so I'm taking her home and Laverne will stay on as chaperone." Or: "Honey, I lost my keys somewhere in the last museum, so can you pick me up?" And even, perhaps, an excited lesbian tourist, once: "Marianne, I just had to call and tell you—the name of Sappho appears on the ceiling in the Great North Hall! Yeah, I took a picture of it! Okay, bye."

But it gnawed at her. Did this ugly old phone even work? It must, if it had not been removed. Of course, it might be that the Library preferred not to make its removal a budget priority this year, letting it sit as a silent testament to recent, outmoded technology. Yes, everything was changing, gradually. She had to update her software more and more, change codes, pass-words, retake training, turn in her cell phone for a new model, the skins of modernization shed and regrown. These were the archivist's tools now: camera, smartphone, laptop, more than the delicate brush restoring a signature or a leather-bound first edition. Everyone younger than Hannah would soon forget, or never know, what it felt like to dial a rotary phone, how long one waited for the nine to roll back, the ridiculous annoyance of trying to dial quickly with a hangnail, with a sprained and splinted finger, with a Band-Aid.

She worked, tried to save money, thought about history and herstory, and waited for a signal from the Overhead. From Sappho. She eagerly awaited the weekend each month when Isabel visited (leaving the bar in the care of a few trusted members), their passionate reunions at National Airport, the first kisses in that great hall and more stolen on the sub-way ride back to Hannah's apartment. Isabel, after that grand year of showing Hannah a whole range of unexpected time-travel experiences, remained cagey and sedate about her powers, rarely introducing them into conversation. But she stocked Hannah's mini-fridge with specially mixed cocktails that enabled them to pursue astounding flights across history during their best lovemaking. They were in Egypt. They were in the Yucatan. They were in the court of Elizabeth, in the court of Kwan Yin, in a speakeasy with flappers.

One night, while watching television during Isabel's late September visit, their legs stretched out on the couch and entwined, toes touching and deliciously stroking one another's ankles, Hannah spotted her Library of Congress notebook under the table lamp. It had randomly flopped open to the page where she'd jotted down that pay phone number. Curiosity fought with comfort: Why sit up now, or move at all, disturbing her lover? They had so little time together. But Isabel was no ordinary lover, as Hannah had discovered rather late in the game of their long friendship and flirtation: She was a mystic as well as a mixologist, a weaver of women's communities, a reader of thoughts. Thus Hannah was not terribly startled when Isabel, without removing her eyes from the old *X-files* rerun on the TV screen, commanded, "Pick up the phone and call that number you're so obsessed with."

Reaching over to her apartment's land-line phone, Hannah dialed experimentally. The number for the Library of Congress ladies' room rang and rang, with neither answer nor disconnect. No burblingly cheerful female robot voice interrupted to advise, "You have reached a non-working number." Huh, thought Hannah. *That ladies' room pay phone is still working. The number's still active. Weird.* She hung up, but oddly, the sound of ringing continued in her ears. *Ring. Ring.*

"Happier now?" asked Isabel, turning away from the television and running her soft, expert fingers over Hannah's cheekbone. They fell back against the temporary cushions of Hannah's temporary apartment, sofa cushions that obediently sailed out from under them to make space for their lovemaking. Sweat beaded under Hannah's breasts. Isabel leaned over her, saying ever so quietly, "I will start at your temples, and move down to your altar, if I may."

The ringing continued, inside Hannah's head.

The first time it happened, Hannah was alone in the restroom washing her hands—sticky from a brown bag lunch of avocado and mango salad—when the pay phone on the wall began to ring. It rang insistently, though not loud enough to attract intervening attention, for no one came running in response, and no other patron/tourist/research scholar emerged from a stall with a hastily straightened skirt to take this call. Hannah looked around in all directions, even peeping under the farthest stall when no one emerged. Meanwhile, the phone kept ringing.

Suddenly, it occurred to Hannah that this call must be for her. It could be from the Overhead Herself. With a final glance around to see if anyone was watching, she reached over to the phone and lifted the heavy black receiver, which rose on a sinewy cord. She could see her own reflection in the metal panels that made up the phone, her face rippling between keypad numbers and printed instructions: *Push # for volume. 4 Minutes for $1.00. Worldwide.* Hannah put the receiver to her left ear. "Hello, this is the Library of Congress," she said, for lack of any better salutation, adding, with an uncontrollable snort of nervous laughter, "And you've reached the women's room."

30

"Yes," a faint voice acknowledged. A faintly English voice. "Can you help me?"

"Who is this?" Hannah demanded. And the bathroom temperature dropped, dropped, as the ghost of Virginia Woolf whispered across the line to Hannah, "Save me. Save me. Save me."

When she came out of the bathroom, her fingers were icy. She touched the elevator button to head back to her office and saw a frosty fingerprint. *How could that be? How could that be Virginia Woolf on the phone?* Woolf had taken her own life. Hannah couldn't bring her back. Was that call placed at the hour of Woolf's drowning? Virginia Woolf had walked into the Ouse River in March of 1941, walked into that cold river with stones in her pockets, leaving behind a suicide note, that made explicit her dread of oncoming madness. *Non compos mentis.* But she also left behind an enormous body of work, revealing her love affairs with women and her frustration with the limits placed on women writers. She had, in *A Room of One's Own*, described the wildly dissimilar privileges accorded male versus female undergraduates at Britain's elite universities. She described being told that as a woman (though in fact the invited guest lecturer that day) she could not walk on the college paths reserved for men. Woolf argued, then, that no woman could fully develop her talents as a writer without a room of her own and an independent income. And then—and then—she went into that river, her body drowned in March, but not found until April. By children.

Hannah shut her eyes against the horror of that moment in history, the loss of a great writer. Woolf had written, in the 1920s, "But how interesting it would have been if the relationship between the two

31

women had been more complicated. All these relationships between women, I thought, rapidly recalling the splendid gallery of fictitious women, are too simple. So much has been left out, unattempted. And I tried to remember any case in the course of my reading where two women are represented as friends . . ." Woolf had fallen in love with Vita Sackville-West, writing in her diary after their first meeting that Vita was "a pronounced sapphist." By 1926, Woolf was sending Vita letters in far less reserved language, desire spilling out of her pen:

> Look here Vita—throw over your man, and we'll go to Hampton Court and dine on the river together and walk in the garden in the moonlight and come home late and have a bottle of wine and get tipsy, and I'll tell you all the things I have in my head, millions, myriads—They won't stir by day, only by dark on the river. Think of that. Throw over your man, I say, and come.

Only by dark on the river . . .

Riding up, shivering, to her office, somewhere between the third and fourth floors Hannah opened her eyes briefly and saw Woolf standing behind her in the elevator, long pensive face clearly reflected in the shiny panel of buttons. Hannah's chilled fingerprint was slowly dissolving, reflected backward at Woolf's breastbone, a fingerprint on Woolf's heart. "Do not bury my books; *they* must be saved," Woolf whispered. "I live on through my body of work now. Can't have another drowning." Hannah whirled around, terrified; no one was there. Then, at the fourth floor, the elevator doors opened and a cheerful party of tourists rushed in, all talking at once, showing off their purchases from the Library bookshop, sorting through handbags and purses. Hannah slipped out, sweat trickling down her lower back into her underwear, heat swiftly returning to her fingertips. *Hot flash or ghost encounter? Does it show?*

Throw over your man, I say, and come.

On the morning of the next day, Hannah thought carefully about how best to use her twenty-minute coffee break. Avoiding the ground-floor bathroom and its pay phone, she took the underground tunnels to reach the Library's newer Madison Building, which housed the Performing Arts Reading Room. Passing the outer exhibits on blueswomen and American jazz artists, she flashed her ID badge and reader identification card at the desk.

"Hi. Ah—do you happen to have any recordings of spoken word? Women poets reading their work aloud? Let's say, oh, how about Virginia Woolf? Anything?"

The young woman on desk duty gave Hannah a smile. "Hell, yeah! But you want the Recorded Sound Collection. Don't worry, you don't need an appointment. I'll take you over." She pushed back her motorized wheelchair with one long hand and came around to Hannah's side of the desk. "Follow me." They walked and wheeled together, toward the climate-controlled Recorded Sound Reference Center. "You're Hannah Stern, right? The archivist. Well, I'm Talia. And I *looove* recorded sound. I do open mic slams."

"It's her voice I'm looking for," Hannah blurted. "Just a feeling that I need to check—to check out the sound of Virginia Woolf's voice. But do we have it here? Anywhere?"

"We have over 3.6 million items—the oldest is about 120 years old, from the earliest moment of recorded sound. Here." Talia pushed herself into the Recorded Sound Research Center, waving her ID. "Today's your lucky day, Hannah. There's just one surviving recording of Woolf's voice, you know. The BBC broadcast it on April 29, 1937, quite a good speech really; it was just one part of a radio series called *Words Fail Me*."

"Brrrr." Hannah shivered now, and it wasn't from the climate control of the archive. "Words did fail her, in the end—failed to comfort her, or give her reason to keep on battling whatever mental illness exhausted her so." She watched in fascination as Talia briskly pulled up the call number of the BBC broadcast and connected fresh headphones to a computer terminal for Hannah. "Damn! We don't have the original here, do we?"

"Oh no, no, it's in Britain, and of course we primarily collect American composers' works. But here, I've brought up the audio file you want right on this computer, so go ahead and have a listen." Seeing the strange angst on Hannah's face, Talia paused. "There's a transcript, too, so you can read along as you hear Woolf talk. I'll just leave you alone with Woolf now," and she backed tactfully away with a brisk wave.

Alone with Woolf. In a few seconds I'll know. I'll know if that really was Woolf's voice I heard on the pay phone and in the elevator. Hannah carefully adjusted the audio headphones, pushed the volume to high, and cued the pages of transcript Talia had loaded for her. *There. As soon as I hear this, I'll know.*

"*Words,*" the voice of Virginia Woolf undulated right into her head.

"Words, English words, are full of echoes, of

memories, of associations—naturally. They have been out and about, on people's lips, in their houses, in the streets, in the fields, for so many centuries . . ." The speech continued, but Hannah's entire body was now pounding with excitement. *It is* her *voice! This* was *Woolf on the phone! She called me! She called me! She called me!*

Then, this line:

"Our business is to see what we can do with the English language as it is," Woolf declared. "How can we combine the old words in new orders so that they survive, so that they create beauty, so that they tell the truth?"

Yes. Save the old words, put them in order, archive the beauty that tells our truths as women who loved women. Was that what she, Hannah, was supposed to do?

That weekend, Hannah exhausted herself combing through Woolf's diaries and letters to find more clues or directives. But the following Monday, as soon as she entered the Library bathroom the pay phone rang and it was Audre Lorde, saying, "Uh huh. What are you doing? You know, poetry is not a luxury."

Every video clip she had access to confirmed the identity of Audre Lorde's voice. Films, conference recordings, speeches: yes, Lorde. Hannah walked in a daze to the Metro, past cafes and coffeeshops where Washingtonians of all stripes looked so normal, so unaware, latte on their lips, the *Post* in their laps, while she, Hannah, played the interior tape loop of that call: *What are you doing?*

The week after that, Hannah answered the buzzing bathroom phone with a panicked outstretched hand and it was Adrienne Rich, whose mere "Hello" dried her mouth into parchment and who instructed, as Hannah's eyes darted around the bathroom (full of women, that day, at the lunch hour), "...the image isn't responsible for our uses of it/it is intentionless/A long strand of dark hair in the washbasin. . . ." A poem from 1969. Hannah had, in fact, heard and met Rich at a poetry conference way, way back in her first year of graduate school, and she knew that poem: "The Photograph of the Unmade Bed," from the collection *The Will to Change*. There wasn't any need to verify that this was Adrienne Rich's voice. When she replaced the phone in its rusting holder, though, she turned around and saw exactly what Rich had described: one long strand of dark hair in the first bathroom sink. Whose? It had not been there before. When the bathroom emptied of tourists for a moment, she wrapped the strand of hair in a paper towel and stuffed it into her briefcase. *Get it tested. But if some scientist tells me it contains Adrienne Rich's own DNA, I'm going to carry goosebumps on my goosebumps for months on end!*

Every week for six weeks a different lost lesbian author called and, it seemed, *ordered* Hannah to do something . . . but what?

Their voices were authentic, that was certain. She marched steadily back and forth in her upscale desert boots to the Recorded Sound Research Center, puzzling the young man there with her weekly requests for live recordings by one lesbian author after another. Through the audio headphones she heard again the tones of Lorde and Rich, and went back to Woolf, all of them contained now on tape. Yet not bound by any conventions of death or time, it seemed.

At home, at night, she jumped out of her skin every time her own phone rang, wondering if the voices would pursue her from her place of work to her cozy little temporary home—but they did not. It was always Isabel on the other end of the line, or, occasionally, her mother. She told neither of them what was happening in her day job.

In a burst of inspiration, however, Hannah did contact the telephone company serving the Mid-Atlantic, hoping to establish when the pay phone had first been installed at the Library of Congress and how long the number had been operational. She had one very important question, though she felt rather frightened to ask it: *who* had owned that phone number before it was assigned to a pay phone? Could a phone number itself have a history? (A woman's history?) But no one seemed to have any information. Three times she was put on hold or disconnected; when she finally reached a recorded message that was in fact comedian Lily Tomlin's voice, snorting, "*We* don't care, we don't have to care, we're the phone company," she realized the Overhead had cut in, gently reminding her to get back to work. A trail of lesbian voices wound like a protective pearl necklace around her search, and she was not meant to hunt for answers yet. She was meant to save books.

Her work was at risk of drowning, Woolf had said. Were her books being thrown into water? Washed away? Buried? *Jewish holy books are buried in sites called a Gineza . . . the Cairo Gineza was the most famous. If lesbian books are sacred to the community I live in, where is our Gineza? Is it the Lesbian Herstory Archives? What happens to our oldest old books? Is Woolf afraid of burial, being buried alive, after drowning?*

This task, this sleuth work, this mission—it was never meant to be "just" a job. The Overhead had not really prepared her. And apparently it wasn't Isabel's role to help her. Hannah was alone, inside the Beltway, inside the Library, inside a bathroom, yet somehow outside time. She'd have to spend the year connecting all the clues, keeping watch while doing her job well, so that no one ever suspected the secret mission that kept her running to the bathroom.

Chapter Two

Very Remote Storage

The first Monday in October, both Washington insiders and alert queers nationwide held their collective breath as the Supreme Court returned to hear cases on LGBT rights and women's reproductive rights, rights that might determine the rest of their lives.

But Hannah's desk at work was piled with folders demanding her full attention. Her little photograph of Isabel had long been knocked askew. "How's it going?" asked Aurora, hurrying by with yet another donor file for Hannah. "Would you mind terribly looking at this one right away? It seems a good collection, and right in your area of expertise. There's some duplication of texts we already own—just indicate where we might sort that out." Hannah sighed, unintentionally blowing an old sheet of onionskin paper into the aisle, and rallied a forced smile for her supervisor as she reached up to accept the bulging folio of documents.

This was a morning of hot flashes, cold coffee, and never-ending assignments. In her former incarnation as a lecturer, life had been simpler, if exhausting: do research for lectures, write the lectures, give the lectures; assign history papers, assist students with rough drafts of papers, grade the finished papers; and meet with students, mentor students, applaud graduating students.

Now her days were filled with the unpredictable: she'd be halfway through one task and abruptly summoned to another, or on her way to take books to one department and then be redirected to a different hall because the First Lady wanted to drop by with an entourage of Chinese dignitaries. The thrill of seeing political celebrities had quickly faded, and the unreliability of the Metro, with its single-tracking repair delays, had made her late for work more than once. She wanted to be a shining star in this universe of protecting women's writings, but was functioning more like a sputtering streetlight. And she missed Isabel, her community, her friends. She finally had a lover and now they were hundreds of miles apart. Moreover, there was that bathroom pay phone to worry about. Had those calls really happened? What, or who, was she supposed to save?

Time for a doughnut. For sure. Not caring that a few rainbow sprinkles fell in a shower onto the folder's cover, Hannah opened the paperwork Aurora had just delivered. It seemed to be a will, or rather a deed of donation. This donor was still living; that usually made things easier. Ah, a list of books. Then Hannah's doughnut fell out of her mouth and rolled away, coming to rest under an old heating unit, where much later it would provide a party for a couple of library mice.

This deed was for two hundred lesbian books. And not just any collection of lesbian books, but a list of nearly every book Hannah herself had read when she was first coming out. How familiar these titles and authors were! There were Naiad Press novels and Rita Mae Brown novels, books by Colette and Karla Jay, Radclyffe Hall and Natalie Barney, Cherie Moraga and Audre Lorde, Bertha Harris and Djuna Barnes, Patricia Highsmith and Christa Winsloe, Lisa Alther and Elsa Gidlow, Monique Wittig and Pat Parker, Judy Grahn and Violette Leduc. And—Hannah gulped—Virginia Woolf! It was like looking at her own rare lesbian bookshelf, some of which she'd brought with her to Washington, and some of which was stored at Isabel's—but with the addition of many unique volumes Hannah had long coveted. This collector also had a goodly range of pulp paperbacks from the 1950s, *Perfume and Pain, That Kind of Love*, and signed editions by children's book author R.R. Knudson. Why would anyone part with such a delicious collection?

The paper deed, itself, felt strangely alive in her hands. And yet she realized with sorrow that this might be a legacy intended for donation because the owner sensed the ending of her life. It might even be someone Hannah's own age, Hannah's generation, now terminally ill but boldly choosing to settle her affairs and secure a place for what she'd valued most: these eye-opening books, the companions of a lifetime.

Was that it? Maybe. Unclear. With a lump in her throat, Hannah realized she had reached the age where her still-young peer group was starting to lose numbers. She already had friends dying of cancer, even battling the warning signs of dementia . . . *And it could be me. I could be next. What am I going to do with* my *stuff, my hundreds of books? Where would they do the most good? Have I thought about that? Taken steps to finish writing my will? But now that I'm with Isabel, what's mine is hers . . .*

She ran to the bathroom and flung herself into a stall. Hot flashes, cold hands. Carefully she palpated

41

each breast. Was that a lump? What about her blood pressure? Heartbeat? She tried to breathe evenly, slowly. Death. Death was a monster and no one got out of here alive. She would soon be dyke dust. Hannah readjusted her sweater and strode to the mirror. Okay, had that mole always been there? Was there more gray hair than usual? How much time did she have? What was her purpose here? *Damn it. Focus.*

Then the pay phone rang. Hannah jumped. There was one other woman in the bathroom, an older security guard, applying fresh makeup; she turned and looked at Hannah, laughing. "Made me jump, too. I didn't even know that old phone worked!"

Thinking fast, Hannah explained, "Oh, right, I told my mother to call me back at this number," and lunged for the phone. The receiver felt icy in her already chilled hands. "Hi, Mom," Hannah croaked, wondering who (or *what*) had placed this call. *Not Mom!*

"Listen, this is important," barked a voice. "Get those books and save 'em. Save them! Are you listening to me? Will you get back to work? And stop staring into the mirror. You look fine; you have decades left. *We* don't have much time. They're going to—" The line went dead.

Hannah worked all morning, through lunch, and by late afternoon was able to collect her thoughts and offer her boss some preliminary suggestions. "Aurora, this is a terrific collection. It practically narrates itself—sort of an arc of coming-out literature. It could easily be a reading list or syllabus from the first generation of lesbian studies in universities and colleges. So, you said that some of these books are already in the Library's archives? If in fact we'll now have doubles, I'd like to propose that we do an exhibit with the duplicates. I can organize that for sure." Hannah was glowing. This must be what she was supposed to do—display the grand range of what publisher Barbara Grier once called *Lesbiana* to a public in need of that history. She was tremblingly certain that had been Grier's own voice on the pay phone, having once phoned the living Grier with a question about the history of women's presses, only to shrink from the barked demand: "Are you kidding? Do you know who you're talking to?"

But now Aurora raised her penciled eyebrows. "Oh, no, I'm afraid not. No displays with anonymous donations, or with this sort of mixed material. It's a good collection, I'll grant you that, but after you catalogue it we have to truck it off-site to our remote storage warehouse in Fort Meade, Maryland. We're that full here. Now, the duplicates we give away, for the Friends of the Library sale."

Off-site? Remote storage? Warehouse in Maryland? Give the duplicates away?

"Oh, dear," said Aurora, realizing Hannah's distress and offering a somewhat patronizing smile. "You didn't think we kept everything here, did you? We have a copy of every book published in the United States. Did you believe all that was shelved right here in the Jefferson and Adams Buildings, in the general collections?"

"Then—where?"

"Oh, shipped from the loading dock to either of our climate-controlled warehouses. There are two remote storage facilities: one at Fort Meade, and one in Landover, Maryland. When researchers want a particular text, they put in a request to the Book Service desk, and we can have it brought in through the twice-daily deliveries from off-site. All perfectly safe and ordinary, and never more than half a day's wait unless a scholar asks very late on Friday night. Of course, more and more we'll be digitizing print, using digital files, and then, thank goodness, we won't need all that space."

"But," Hannah heard herself fumbling for words, "don't those books, kept out there where no visitors ever go, get lonely? Unseen . . . sort of waiting . . . you know. What if no one ever requests them? A lifetime in confinement, in *Landover.*" *And maybe that was it. Buried alive in a warehouse, waiting to be loved again. Woolf?*

Aurora sat down. "I may be a bit less attached than you, after all these years of cataloguing, but I assure you: the point of both a public library *and* a research library is to give readers what they seek, even if it's distasteful to us," and she glanced at the donor's list of lesbian pulp paperbacks, featuring titles like *The Evil of Friendship* and *Call Me Pet!* "We don't keep books to be merely decorative. Each imparts knowledge. However, in any library, there is what is called 'weeding,' or taking a book out of circulation. For example, a public library may order twenty copies of a current bestseller when patrons are making a run on that title, and then after some time there are eighteen copies never touched again. Some books may never have been checked out by any reader at all. At a certain point, these unused duplicates are taken out of circulation and crated for a Friends of the Library book sale, and what's left from that sold to a third-party book distributor, or donated to prison libraries." Again, she glanced disdainfully at the donor sheet, and added, "Of course, most prisons would not accept these books. The content is too sexual, and some of it boldly felonious, no?"

Great. Forget about getting lesbian literature to les-

44

bians behind bars. Hannah's bitter response was, "So libraries would throw out rare paperbacks rather than donate them to women who want them?" She pointed to one title. "One person's pornography is another's breakthrough novel about being different."

Aurora sighed, tucking a lock of hair into her sweeping updo. "You're quite right. But brace yourself for many difficult decisions of, ah, separation. When books come in that are damaged, we have to make certain decisions. If a damaged cover is made of old materials that can be sewn, that goes to Cataloguing for repair. But books that can't be mended, or have obvious mold, are recycled." She took in Hannah's blank look. "Sent to the *shredder,*" she emphasized, and then stood up and quickly walked away.

She couldn't relax. Watching the evening news from the Supreme Court docket didn't help: homophobia still the official rule of law in so many states, gay kids jumping off bridges, idiot school superintendents forbidding LGBT sensitivity training or curricula on diversity. *Heather Has Two Mommies* had just been banned for the umpteenth time. Impulsively, Hannah walked over to where her own copy of that book lay atop her redwood bookshelf and gave the cover a kiss. "Kiss where it hurts," she murmured. She was almost certain the book had kissed back, and was about to pour herself a stiff drink, when Isabel called.

It was the usual time they had agreed to call each other every night. But when Isabel sang into the phone, "What time is it?" she meant something else. Hannah shivered with pleasurable anticipation. This was an invitation to phone sex. In any century she liked.

And how it was possible, how Isabel sent both of

45

them to such places on command, she did not know. She had promised to stop asking after last year's many miracles of time travel. Isabel had introduced her, had *sent* her, to the great and the everyday women of the past: one unexpected journey every month. Hannah would be at the bar celebrating some holiday event with the women of her own community and suddenly be in ancient Israel, in ancient Lesbos, in the castle of a pirate queen, on the Underground Railroad, or in World War II or a cavewoman's birthing chamber. Thus Hannah learned that in loving Isabel, she was dating a witch. *But how does it work?*

Never mind. It had been a long day. She lay down on the couch, barefoot and topless, just a warm towel wrapped around her midsection, and closed her eyes. "Hello, babe," she murmured into the phone. "Take me back to England, seventeenth or eighteenth century. I'm a buxom serving wench and you're the clever pastry cook at the castle." She heard Isabel laugh; even better, she began to *feel* Isabel's time-travel magic warming up. "Here we go," Hannah urged. "Please, Isabel. Take me there. And feed me."

The next day, her inner fire restored by hours of excellent phone sex and time travel, Hannah confronted her supervisor over the fate of the book donation. "Look, Aurora—why would this donor's books be sent off-site to very remote storage? I know so many women in the community who would love to see them on exhibit." *Or read them, or reread them, or discover them anew . . . and then there are all those schoolkids whose libraries banned* Heather Has Two Mommies . . . *their only chance of seeing a book like that is if they come here and see an exhibit!*

"My dear romantic, we simply don't have room

anymore. This donor has willed us what appear to be additional copies of, yes, certain worthy originals we already do have somewhere in our LGBT collection. We're bursting at the seams. It's not, ah, personal." Aurora sniffed.

More kindly she explained, "If you investigate any of the LGBT archives now well past their early years, they too are victims of their own success. How many early editions of Judy Grahn can your Lesbian Herstory Archives fit on its limited shelf space in Brooklyn? Yes, of course I know about that archive, and support its mission. So many donors have left disorganized collections that every archive has to use a storage unit until the gold can be sorted from the mold," and she smiled, well pleased with her little joke. Noticing that Hannah's expression did not change, she added, "I know everything on this list may seem like gold to you."

"It's not just that—it seems a tragic waste that duplicate first edition copies are given away. You told me that extras are designated for sales or institutions. Can't I take them? Put them in the right hands?"

"I'm afraid not. We checked this list against what we already have, and packed the best books for temporary storage off-site. They'd already be in the loading dock. We culled some others meant for our annual sale, but that won't happen until spring, and that carton is secured for now. Your job is cataloguing what we'll store off-site, no more, no less." A pause. Then Aurora looked over her glasses and said, "Again, I can promise that these works are gradually being digitized. And I assure you, both present and future generations will have the same access to them that you and your . . . friends have enjoyed and, I am well aware, valued. But we must make space for that digital age by downsizing our actual collections, especially," she chuckled to herself again, "when the gold *acquires* mold. So, out with paper, and onto Kindle, yes? You just can't hold on to everything, my dear."

Yes, I can! Yes, I have to!

Hannah sat at her desk through lunch, fuming through mouthfuls of sandwich and mercilessly tearing apart a soft pumpkin spice muffin. She could actually feel her molecular structure shift and change, superimposing the wits and stance of fictional girl detective characters over her body. She was Velma. She was Nancy Drew. She had to get to that loading dock and stop that donation from being tagged for very remote storage. But as she chewed her way into a possible plan of action, Hannah paused to consider her own words. *Aurora calls it "remote storage." I keep saying "very" remote storage. How come?*

What would "very" remote storage be?

The afterlife? Where our memories go?

It was another week before Hannah found time in her afternoon break to seek out the loading dock. By then, she had catalogued a list of the rare lesbian books the donor intended for Capitol Hill visitors, books that were instead going into exile in Landover. With no plan beyond a vague idea of rescue, she headed out and inward, taking sideways passages up and down floors, over and through the different "cores" of the Library, into and out of elevators, greeting no one, her face buried in a brochure on presidential cookbooks. In this manner she reached the back loading dock, where crates of books waited in stoic silence, destined either for careful off-site shipment—or the shredder.

It was a noisy, masculine space. Men in protective support belts lifted and shoved book crates into cargo vans that backed up to the doors. Other workers were moving what looked like broken furniture, dented files, and other materials long past their prime to an area marked for trash pickup and recycling. Damaged and old books were visible on both sides: some destined for donation, others for garbage.

Out with the old, the unusable, the extra, the past. *Huh. That's how my community is starting to feel . . . remaindered in the bin of culture.* Trying to look like she had every right to be there on official Library business, her ID clipped front and center on her goddess necklace, Hannah wandered over to the aisles of old equipment marked for recycling—and froze.

A *glue machine!* She'd worked on one during that terrible second year of graduate school, when the teaching assistants were rotated into library service at the university. For complicated reasons of budget and personnel, Hannah was assigned to glue card holders onto the backs of incoming books. It was a winter of hot glue, burns, her fingers sticking together, and the smell of paste. Unavoidably sniffing library paste and hot glue all day, she'd reel home, high, and try to read history.

Here was the old machine itself, or an elaborate cousinly version, slated for permanent vacation—no longer gluing cards for readers' names. *Where are all those old cards? What if someone has them? I bet there are some pretty famous names—authors, scholars, politicians who came in to do research here—if those cards could talk!* She was about to give the machine an affectionate pat when she noticed the long open box of books nestled underneath it.

Someone had lodged part of the donor's lesbian paperback collection here—designating the perfectly good books for shredding, not even off-site storage or sale. These books were now on death row with other

49

trash materials. How? Why? Tears filled Hannah's eyes at the thought: what crime had they committed? What if their generous donor could see their undignified fate?

And the oddest thing happened next. Hannah's ears heated up. She clutched at the flaming hot left side of her head, sending her woman's symbol earring flying. Was she having an allergic reaction to the dust of ages—something here in the cavernous space?

Then the tickling heat became a murmur in her ears and, finally, a soundtrack in her head. She was hearing the box of books, weeping.

Save us! the books cried, a chorus of thin papery voices. *We're being digitized out of existence! Don't let them shred us! Don't send us to Shreddy, the Evil One! Get us to new owners, the ones who never knew us, never had us. Let us start anew, relationships of promise, mutual love. We're becoming unglued just when we yearn to be checked out by young dykes!*

Hannah whipped around to see if someone was behind her, playing some prank, or watching her at this peculiar emotional moment. No; she was alone. Quite a few of the Library workmen had just left for lunch. She dropped to her knees, hands over her ears.

Save us!

It hurt. It hurt to hear, to feel the pain in that flat cry of anguish. This was a rescue mission now, she was certain: she had to save these books. And how would that work? Stuff them under her blouse, two at a time, and hide them somewhere else? She knew from her weeks of work that all visitors and staff submitted their bags to be searched before leaving the Library itself. There was no way to smuggle the donor's valuable collection into Hannah's apartment. She'd have to move these books somewhere else *within* the building, at least until she figured out what in hell she

50

was supposed to do. She'd have to get them out a few at a time when workmen weren't paying attention.

Shreddy, the Evil One! What could that mean? Books separated out to be shredded went to some local recycling facility, along with, most likely, various government documents. That shredder would be a nightmare figure for any aging book longing to be held and read rather than destroyed. For authors, too, aging out—or dead. What could be more of a foe than the cold machinery of government tearing into a woman's literary opus, rendering it unreadable? It would be a second death. And suddenly Hannah, too, could see that big, indifferent mechanical body, the eight-armed machine chewing up books and drooling ink. Shreddy was an octopus, a monster who leaked ink when poked, a rare book at the end of every tentacle, hungry for more.... More ...

Then, as Hannah reached out with one trembling hand to pick out three books, it was the distinct voice of Virginia Woolf she heard saying, "More." *More books to save? Another box? Where?*

The rumbling start of an engine gave the answer. *It must already be loaded on a truck!* Still holding three books, Hannah ran to the back loading dock area. There! The off-site storage truck! Its sliding back door still raised, it yawned carelessly open, revealing the many stacked boxes all labeled and destined for remote storage. *Too remote!* the books in her hand cried thinly. *Burial. Get us back!*

The two or three men working nearby all had their backs to her, distracted and busy, moving a splintered desktop to a side wall. No time to feel guilt, betrayal of her position at the Library, disloyalty to her boss; no time to feel anything but action in service to the Overhead and the world of girls. Without any further plan, Hannah jumped into the truck.

There were so many boxes it was hard to focus her eyes. The truck's interior was humid and close after the climate-controlled Library. She fingered and read the edges of labels until she found what she was looking for. *Aha! Donation, J.M. Off-site.* At least fifty of the best books from the donor's collection had been culled, thankfully not for destruction, but instead designated for exile at the Landover facility.

Hannah crouched down, marveling that such jewels of rare lesbian literature would now be hidden from public view until requested by a lone, persistent scholar such as herself, or some future graduate student curious to look at a paperback original. No young people, pre-credentialed, would ever enter that facility to browse and fondle and select and breathe in the books, or encounter them accidentally in a life-changing moment.

The vintage paperbacks would rot, unloved, in a digital age. It felt eerily like that final scene in *Raiders of the Lost Ark,* Indiana Jones locating the Ark of the Covenant containing the dust of the Ten Commandments tablets, nobly handing it off to a wartime U.S. government for study by federal scientists only to have the Ark vanish forgotten into an infinite secret warehouse.

Hannah's covenant was with The Overhead. *She* wanted these books placed in the hands of women and girls now. That was one of Her commandments. There were urgent needs of readers now, now, and not only now but *then, then.* Hannah was tasked with getting these books back to the past. But how was that arrangement supposed to unfold? No time to feel anything. The clock was ticking.

The slamming of the truck's rear door sent her

heart pounding anew. "Okay, Al," shouted a masculine voice. And the engine roared to life. The wheels turned, and with lurching forward movement they pulled away from the Library of Congress. She was shut tight in the cargo van, buried inside with the locked books, all of them bound for remote storage in Maryland.

Hannah's first thought was that she was about to lose another job: first she'd be missed at work, then discovered stealing. Or could she spin this ridiculous moment into a complaint of kidnapping and emerge heroic? No, not likely. Should she bang on the truck wall and alert the driver to her predicament? What if that startled "Al" into driving right up a tree?

Lunch hour. Lunch hour: that was her only hope. Maybe, just maybe, Al had tossed back a strong coffee or two, necessitating a bathroom stop before they pulled onto the Beltway and the point of no return. Maybe a strong brew . . . And the mere word, *brew,* sent a vision of Isabel into her head. Her lover, the mixologist, the brewster.

She squeezed her eyes shut. In her mind she saw Isabel at the bar, capably sifting the named and unnameable herbs and ingredients into their drinks, serving just what each customer needed on a Friday night at Sappho's Bar and Grill. She saw Isabel reach for the golden coffeemaker under the counter, where it was always ready to treat the sober or the sleepy who preferred caffeine to gin, and now Isabel pulled from her canvas apron pocket a little bag of magic beans—beans that somehow laughed at the limitations of ordinary time and space, first ground to finest powder at Sappho's, and earlier today showing up in the coffeepot of a loading dock in Washington.

Al, honest and hardworking, his daily drives back and forth to the Landover warehouse to deposit or fetch books made bearable with crime books on tape and strong coffee. Al, his mind soothed to the point of bliss on magic bean coffee, cheerfully forgetting to lock the back of the truck after closing it shut; Al turning the wheel to leave Capitol Hill and going no further than a block or two before the coffee in his veins dove for an exit; Al realizing a bathroom break was in order, now pulling sharply to a stop at the first gas station on the right, and, after locking the cab of the van, heading into the men's room, keys jingling faintly on his belt.

When she could no longer hear that jingle, Hannah pulled the crate of books onto one of several upright dollies leaning against the truck's interior wall and crouched at the back door, frantically surveying it for the handle to open the back. It *did* open! He *had* forgotten to lock it! Now she had, what, four minutes to escape? If Al were the constipated sort . . . but what if several people saw, and reported, the dyke emerging from a library van with a crate on a dolly and racing into the adjacent neighborhood?

But no one saw. And no one ever reported what was surely one of the odder moments, that hour, at a gas station that had seen many an oddity through the Watergate years, the Iran-Contra scandals, the protest marches on Washington.

Because as Hannah pushed open the van's back doors and dumped out a crate and a dolly, then heaved herself out and locked the van doors again securely, the Overhead's Projector beamed down a cloud of light that briefly blinded everyone but Hannah. And when she had pulled the crate on the dolly around the corner and out of sight, racing toward the nearest Metro stop, the light faded at the gas station in time for a pleasant-faced man to step out of the restroom, and get back in his truck, noticing nothing amiss, never reporting one missing box and one lost dolly. The magic coffee beans were purged and flushed to the Potomac.

Gasping, the sweat of adrenalin plastering her bangs to her forehead, Hannah pulled the treasure-crate of books behind her until she reached Eighth Street SE. There, silent behind its screen of obscuring plywood frontage, was the oldest continually operating lesbian bar in America—even older than Sappho's, and now about to close—Phase One.

Here, generations of lesbians had lifted a brew to the love that dared not speak its name. Olivia Records had been planned nearby, too, and over the years other lesbian arts bloomed here, from poetry slams to drag king shows. It was empty now, readying for closure and then sale, its glory days past. Though the Phase was typically locked at midday, Hannah knew one barkeep who might be there. The counterpart to Isabel in D.C. was Miss Luna.

She pressed the bell now, calling, "Luna! Help. I need you. Can you open up?" And Luna yelled, "We're *closed*; this Phase is *over*," but she came clumping to the door, towering and mighty in her Fluevog shoes. She saw Hannah standing there in rumpled, van-streaked work clothes, clenching a book dolly, and burst into wise laughter. "What the hell?"

"Hi. I can't explain now, but can I stow these books behind the bar for two hours? I'll come get them at five, when I'm off work." Hannah's eyes were pleading. "Can you stay here until five, and let me in?"

Luna stood with hands on hips, considering.

"I've got a vintage vampire doll for you," was Hannah's bribe.

"Hmmm." Smiling eyes granted assent, a hand seized the dolly, and the door bolted shut again. No passerby paused or even indicated they had seen the exchange. Too many deals, both drug and political, had been sealed on that long block in days and years gone by. Too many men had learned it was best not to acknowledge anything that went on at the doorway to Phase One.

Hannah ran eight blocks back to the Library, panting and laughing simultaneously, and then pulled up behind a tree to reassemble herself. With face blank and work ID clipped forward, she went right back to work in the Jefferson Building, nodding to Aurora as she returned the files she had been sent to go retrieve an hour ago. "Got lost, did you?" snapped Aurora, busy with accounts now, failing to notice that Hannah's entire rear end was coated with shipping sawdust. Hannah apologized and sat down quickly, her mind racing. *Okay. I'll get those books home, and then . . . then wait for instructions. I'll keep them under my bed until spring. That's what I'll do. And not tell anyone.*

So it was that on a pleasant weeknight, the first Tuesday in October, as Capitol Hill law clerks and staff interns excitedly argued the new cases on the Supreme Court's docket, no one paid much attention to a middle-aged lesbian pulling a box onto the Metro with a dolly. Half of the commuters boarding at Capitol South similarly dragged law files or locked plastic organizers on small rolling baggage carts. Everyone took work home here; there was no such thing as a night off in Washington. It was, in that way, like graduate school, another subculture permanently stamping its participants with the ethic that all-time-is-work-time and there's no-such-thing-as-a-weekend. Of course, the worker bees here in Washington were charged with running the nation. Academics doing scholarship 24/7 were rarely credited with any mission beyond radicalizing campus.

Anyway, Hannah knew the Metro ride home might be the only "free" time anyone had between workday and an evening bent over government files. She looked with interest as bureaucrats' personalities emerged in the shared anonymity of underground transportation. Women bent down, exchanging fashion heels for padded athletic shoes, sighing with relief; others plugged in headphones or attacked a crossword puzzle. Books emerged from shoulder bags: *The Handmaid's Tale*, the Bible, the Koran. Some passengers were praying with closed eyes; others were playing *Bejeweled* on cell phones. No one spared a glance for Hannah's crate of iconic lesbian lit. Everyone had their own eccentricity here, shaking off a day's toil at the Department of Agriculture.

How many commuters also led secret lives, like Hannah? What was *really* in all those other rolling files? What if the Metro suddenly ground to a halt—in fact, it often did—and they lived out the rest of their lives as a group? Who would emerge as a startling hero or villain in that story? As Hannah smiled at the woman beside her, she wondered who among these companions journeying underground might also be a Sappho, or The Overhead, in disguise.

Chapter Three

Bibliophilia

Halloween weekend found Hannah back in her old university town, reunited with her lover and her old pals at Sappho's Bar and Grill. Though painfully aware she was no longer a professor at the local university, which had been her employer and home for so many years, Hannah grinned in pleasure as gentle banter greeted her from all sides when she arrived at the bar on Friday, October 30. "Yo! It's Dr. Stern! The bureaucrat!" "Not too fancy to drink with us, now, I hope?" "Got any Beltway insider tips? Can you please fix the government?" "What about that hot new dyke senator, what's-her-name? Have you had a two-martini lunch with her yet? Aw, why not?"

Oh, old friends! My bar, my gang, my tribe! Her heart melted. Was there anything better in the world than old dyke pals of long standing, the ones whose teasing was like the rough caress of a cat's tongue, every bristle an intimate familiarity, a stroke of trust and love? What ingredients coalesced into such perfect/imperfect community? She looked around, taking note of the simple elements: bar stools, pool table, decorations, sound booth.

But at the center, the mystic who made it possible: Isabel, her lover, whose drinks could free the bonds of time and space, or cure your cold, or make you face the fears of a past era. They had so little time together, now that Hannah was in Washington for a year, yet their time was fluid. They had known one another as friends since graduate school days. They had become lovers only last New Year's Eve, when events strange and wondrous had revealed Isabel to be a time traveler and manifester of time travel for Hannah. That recent winter and spring, when they were finally intimate partners, had included lovemaking so breathless and tender that now Hannah was startled into spontaneous moans when she looked back on their first months.

Isabel had made love to her while murmuring in Latin, in Greek, in Aramaic. On those nights (and afternoons), beads of syllables clung like moisture to the ornate mirror in Isabel's bedroom and dripped back onto them. Isabel wrote love letters with fingers wet from Hannah's arousal and those letters somehow stayed fully formed in the air, stiffening into sugar icing and then breaking apart to fall into their mouths like parachutes of candy.

Tonight, Isabel said little as she apportioned the magic beverages that kept women coming back for the taste of womanspace, the flavor of community. Just now she stood behind the bar, smiling and pouring drinks from the particular witches' cauldron she utilized only at Halloween. The first round was free to the first thirteen bar regulars. But, Hannah noted with perplexed admiration, the drinks were all completely different in appearance as they flowed into each valued patron's glass. Silver, cider, foaming, wine-red, green. No one remarked on this, having long ago accepted that their bartender trafficked in the unusual—that they, themselves, might be unusual too, a charmed and charming circle of lesbian lives that had landed here, at Sappho's Bar and Grill, for this historical time frame. However, after a few sips, as blue-jeaned bottoms settled back on leather-topped stools, Moira chose to speak.

"Mmm. Wasn't it that first Mary Poppins book where the kids took their evening medicine in different colors and flavors from the same bottle? And then it turned into rum punch for Poppins? I always loved those books." Isabel said nothing, but used the ice tongs in her hand to point out a faded *Mary Poppins* volume on the glass-encased bookshelf behind the bar.

They each sipped their drinks and sighed in private, separate satisfaction. "What was your favorite book as a kid, Letty?" Hannah asked, and the bar butch who proudly claimed the longest association with Sappho's released a startled sneeze. Everyone waited expectantly. "Why, I don't know. Yeah, I do know. It was about the life of Helen Keller. We had a deaf-blind cousin my age, stuck away up at the state institution. Probably smart as a whip, but it was the Depression, her mama had no money and no child support and nobody knew anything about anything. That kid had absolutely no rights, let me tell you. They took her away right after her eighth birthday.

"Well, I got this book and taught myself finger spelling and went up to the Institute on the nickel trolley and told Maggie I'd take care of the doll family, and I smuggled one doll into her mattress. But after that . . . shit. Don't even know what happened to her, where she is now, and she was my own flesh and blood." Letty blew her giant nose.

"Jeez, Letty," Moira objected. "Thanks for the real cheerer-upper. Although who knew you taught yourself sign language as a kid? You've been holding out on us. What else don't we know about you? There's obviously more to you than your secret ability to win at pool every time." Letty finger-spelled, "Tough titty. Not telling."

"Um," began Hannah, already woozy from the effect of one of Isabel's "special" potions, "I guess I've been hoping to ask all of you this question. What was the first book any of you took out from a library? And did a librarian help you? Or treat you badly?"

"Treat me badly? Hell, no. I was in love with my school librarian," Trale asserted, jiggling her long legs against the floorboards. *Miss Diane.* I took out every book they had just to see her over and over: nature books, bugs, maps and atlases. She'd say, 'Why, it's you, my little bookworm!' and I'd just be crazy with love. Later on, I figured, huh. She was well over thirty and not married. Probably spotted a kindred spirit there, but who knows? She was nice." Trale sighed.

"I know what you're getting at, Hannah," Yvette added. "Isabel told me you got obsessed with those libraries that refused to lend books to black children. Well, that didn't happen to me. I grew up in Brooklyn. But it was a different kind of racism—a race pride focus, with well-meaning folks discouraging your taste for anything else, anything they found frivolous. My youth leader tried to get us to take out books on Africa and Malcolm X and I was interested in, ah, well, becoming a Broadway actress . . ."

"*You?*" everyone screamed. Yvette was now the grants and fundraising manager for the public television station, famous for never once appearing on the air throughout many years of holiday membership drives.

"... but the book that changed me, if y'all will just *shut up,* was *The Snowy Day.* It had a black child in the snow in the city and hardly any words. I could read it, and that child looked like my brothers, and like me. I know that later, when I started at WSRP, I wanted to be damn sure that other black kids saw kids like themselves on TV, in formats that pushed them to read early. So I figured, hell, I'll fundraise for shows like *Sesame Street* that were mixed racially. I mean, I grew up with Morgan Freeman on *The Electric Company* teaching kids word skills!"

Tongues loosened. More women arrived and were offered the Halloween special (though no longer for free.) Certain couples had broken up and re-formed in new ways since Hannah left town, but all seemed cheerful and civil to one another, and the freshly aligned sweethearts pounded Hannah on the back, grabbed an autumn-hued beer or two, and joined in the conversation.

"*Harriet the Spy*," a group of women decreed. "Best baby-dyke book ever."

"Sure, if you identified with living on the Upper East Side of Manhattan, going to an exclusive prep school, and having a live-in nanny and a cook," Dog argued. "Same with *Eloise*. I liked *Little House on the Prairie*. Everyone worked hard in that house."

"But it was so hostile to the Native Americans—how could I relate to it? Or to any of that genre of pioneer books white girls loved? *Caddie Woodlawn, Bread-and-Butter Journey,* ay," Shoni protested. "I had to make do with the tiresome Sacajawea and Poca-hontas biographies. Not even my nation!"

"What about books that made it okay just to be eccentric? Or sorta independent? Or just a girl get-ting in trouble? *Pippi Longstocking, Amelia Bedelia, Madeline.*"

"Here's what confuses me," Yvette interjected. "By the time you're like, fourteen, or even twelve, you got the vague idea that some characters seemed kinda gay, and maybe some authors were kinda gay because they kept introducing these tomboy chicks. Nancy Drew had that pal named George, and then there was Peppermint Patty and her sidekick Marcie in all the Peanuts collections I owned. But what started the stereotype that librarians are gay? Not all of them are, you know."

"Just all the ones I've ever met," from Trale.

Letty slammed down her glass, sending foam onto Hannah's eyelashes. "My sister and I were on this just the other night. She said, the one career that shouts out queer whether you're a man or a woman is librarian. Now why is that?"

Instant responses from all over the bar, at the pool table, and from someone apparently already lying down under the pool table. "Because you like books better than sports, if you're a dude!" "Because it's a sissy thing to be a boy bookworm!" "Because real men play football after school—they don't go home and read *Jane Eyre.*"

"And," Trale added quietly, "if you're a woman, it's the idea that you prefer a book to a man. You'd rather take a book to a restaurant than a male date. You're an educated woman so you don't need a husband. In fact, what man would have you? You probably smell like library paste."

"No, you smell like books, which is a totally different vibe," argued Dog. "You have that great leather and paper and ink huff going on." She leaned over and sniffed Hannah's neck. "Like you. This," and she swooned.

"Watch it," warned Isabel, sweeping Dog's tips off the bar with a capable forearm. Then the door banged open, and all eyes turned as Theodora walked in—one dark eyebrow slightly raised, legs that seemed to glide rather than ambulate. Her athletic spectacularness only mildly compromised by the bag of ice plastic-wrapped around one lean thigh, she pulled off the lanyard holding her Fox 40 whistle and officiating ID and tossed it on the bar. "Well, that sucked. I had to stop the game and call a foul on my ex tonight. Yep, held up a red card right in her pert little face!"

"Hannah wants to know, what was your favorite book as a kid, and did some librarian ever mess you up?" yelled Letty, now standing in line for the bathroom.

Theodora looked puzzled. "Can't a referee get drunk first?"

"Try drinking before the match, your officiating might improve," and Dog, a veteran of many local tournaments, beat it out the door just in time to avoid a firm swat on her behind. Trale went up to the sound booth and put on dance music as several women, feeling the heat of pre-Halloween libations on a Friday night, suddenly needed to cut loose. But Theodora saw Hannah and smiled, then limped over to sit beside her, ice bag dripping. "Are you back? Just here for the weekend? Taking a survey for your job in D.C.?"

"No, just—interested," Hannah shouted over strains of Poly Styrene and Annie Lennox. "Dora, did you have jock books as a girl?"

"*Babe Didrikson, Girl Athlete,*" recited the community's beloved referee. "That subtitle made it seem like she was this exotic plant or disease. A living peculiarity, like *Girl Lamp Post.* And it was illustrated in sickly industrial green, a color not found in nature. I gave up and read horse books."

Isabel was taking a quick break from serving, allowing Moira to run the cash register, and joined the conversation at the bar. "Hannah, anyone who grew up in our time was unlikely to get a children's book with a lesbian character or a gay family. We invented what we needed. Most of us found our first 'gay' book when we were in junior high or high school, and it was usually a book meant for adults, not young adults. Thankfully all that's changing now. You can get *Heather Has Two Mommies, Annie on My Mind.*"

"Yeah, right—through mail order!" Shoni disagreed. "My boarding school banned anything like that. We had censorship at the town library, too—some group called 'Parents Aware' decreed that if they had a gay book display, there had to be an exhibit representing the *other side* of the 'issue.' We knew that was a crock of shit. If you put out civil rights lit, were you obliged to put a Klan reading list next to it for 'balance' of viewpoint? But rather than be 'balanced' they put all the gay literature behind the counter, and you had to have your parents' permission. Of course, all the Native kids at boarding school were far away from our parents. We pooled our money and paid off one white girl to take out *Even Cowgirls Get the Blues.* That had a part-Siwash character and a great lesbian sex scene, and we passed that around the dorm."

Everyone who had ever owned a smuggled copy of *Cowgirls* in their coming-out years now sighed and began reciting from various passages. "Teeth of foam, lips of pie." "O why is it always so difficult between women?" "Long, thick tongues painted each other . . ."

"You know," Hannah mused, "I really learned to be a lesbian from books. I didn't know anyone like me, or so I thought. I didn't have a clue what women did, or how it might work, or what it ought to feel like."

"Weren't you ever on a softball team?" Theodora inquired sympathetically.

". . . and some books just plain aroused me," Hannah continued, ignoring Dora's usual dig at her lack of athletic pedigree. "I mean, come on. Colette, Anais Nin . . ."

"Oh, all that, the soft soft soft porn Europeans," Yvette snorted. "Show me where in those works there's any real fucking going on!"

"But if you're just awakening and not even ready for it? Colette made my head spin. Then my other parts. 'I listened for a long time to what her mouth told mine.' That was enough, to start. It worked, for me," Hannah argued. "I wanted to be a writer *and* have a female lover. The interwar Europeans showed me a world where women chose both, even before my time."

"*We* had to make do with peeking at medical textbooks," said Letty, puffing as she came off the dance floor to rejoin the conversation.

"Jane Rule did it for me. That look into lesbian identity, without much explicit sex description," Dora agreed with Hannah. "Those were books you didn't have to worry about leaving around, because if you had snoopy friends or parents, they'd have to flip through many a page to find actual censor-worthy passages. Yet there are such great lines, *great* lines there. But just when you think you're going to learn what lesbians do in private, the next page is all about conflict and morality and anguished relationship drama."

"That *is* what lesbians do," Moira put in.

They all began quoting from various Jane Rule novels. "Talk to desire, make it come to you." "So that breasts do not forget what thighs open for now." "Her mouth came down hard on mine as if to answer." "After that night . . . which had no sequel . . ." Laughter and toasts followed each quote, each memory.

"I don't know," sighed Letty, chin on fist. "I was more in sync with that Jill Johnston, who says in

Lesbian Nation that when she was out in Greenwich Village in the late '50s, 'There was no lesbian identity. There was lesbian activity.' All those lesbian publishers and presses came after I paid my dues. Y'all were real lucky." She poked Hannah with her beer.

"We loved anything that made us real," Trale added, getting up again to dance. "We always do. The question is whether what we love, loves us back in kind, whether those books felt the heat that came off our sweating palms. The heat of first discovery, then home-coming, then genre." Hannah picked up her pen to write this down, and Isabel knocked it out of her hand, and ordered her to dance.

The next day Hannah thought about those conversations as she and Isabel swept the bar and readied it with decorations and treats for the real Halloween party and dance that night.

There was so much love for the books that had, in whatever large or limited way, helped them find a lesbian identity, a validation. Too many women had to make do with "banned" lesbian books or scary medical encyclopedia entries on homosexuality.

And then along came Hannah's students, who could download everything ever written about gay and lesbian books at the touch of a computer button, their own treasure hunts (whether personal or academic) for books and images about kids like themselves supported by search engines, databases, social media, gay and lesbian archives. Hannah felt most at home with those in her age group, last of the baby boomers, who had come out in the heady days of the lesbian cultural movement when women's bookstores filled the aching gap, providing discovery and delight on shelves stacked with both classic and recent lesbian volumes that called out: *This is where we are. Hiya, kid. We were waiting for you.*

The biggest generation chasm was between women like Letty, who grew up poor with no opportunity to go to college in an era when no one said the word *lesbian,* and Hannah's most recent students, who had always inhabited a world of gay rights and gay books online, and who were starting to regard Hannah's generation of woman-only bookshops as transphobic quaintness.

Competing ideas and generational conflicts swirled through Hannah's mind as she pinned up crepe paper, polished Isabel's witch cauldrons, and cleaned sticky shot glasses left over from the previous night. Those early, odd books that different women had stumbled across in their search for identity—was it possible that those books knew how important a role they'd played in so many young women's awakening? *Your book saved my life. I thought I was the only one.*

Hannah winced and shrugged as she recalled she'd written a few letters like that herself, to authors who had made an impact on her life, her self-awareness. Now she occasionally received such letters herself, carefully preserving them in bound folios.

But did the anxiously thumbed, hungrily read, sometimes even stolen life-changing *books, themselves,* know they were so loved? Could cloth and paper feel the urgent sweating palms of teenage bookworms? Was there an accumulated deposit of need and angst and relief built up between the lines from every baby dyke who ever checked out or pawed through that one copy of Rita Mae Brown in the midsized town library? What if those books could speak of what they'd seen? *Aha,* Hannah grinned, setting decks of tarot cards out on the bar and positioning the lavender Ouija board near the make-out sofa. *There's a good title. "If these books could talk."* She saw herself at fourteen, hovering in front of the 301 section of the Little Falls Library, confused and embarrassed because her family phone number area code then was also 301, and she'd felt marked. The lesbian-feminist books two local librarians had enthusiastically stocked in those late 1970s years seemed to leer at her: *We know where you live, kid! Yeah, 301 is your neighborhood, isn't it? We got your number, all right. Start reading us now, you'll be writing us later! Ahahahaha!*

She closed her eyes, remembering. As she saw herself at fourteen, nervously looking for books about "tomboys," one of her classmates appeared just one aisle over, in that very library. It was—it was—could that actually be Jordan Matthews, who once wrote in everyone's yearbook, "Have a great summer, and don't go queer like Hannah Stern!," caught in the act of lifting a copy of *Our Bodies, Ourselves?* Wait a minute—what was she, so smug and religious, doing in the 301 section? Could it be that Jordan, too, had been like Hannah? And if so, was—

"It looks great in here, my love," Isabel broke into Hannah's daydream. "You can go back to my place now and rest up for tonight, or get some work done, or try on your costume: anything you like. I'll be busy here for one more hour, then home to cook you dinner. Witches' brew."

Hannah waited in Isabel's apartment, weak with longing. Would it be like her last visit? Lovemaking as a musical score, bars of music replacing the bedspread beneath them, sex in double time, quarter time, all the time they conjured? *Time.* With the change in Hannah's work, they made do with these weekends and holidays, and inevitably it would be

Sunday afternoon closing in on Sunday evening, and the long drive away or trip to the regional airport loomed.

Hannah would stand weeping against Isabel's breasts, raging: "There's not enough time."

Like now: the weekend half over and much of it spent working at the bar. Well, she was involved with a bar owner. What did she expect? And not just any bar. And Halloween, not just any night.

Hannah sat down in what she already thought of as "their" bedroom, clean and ready for the party that night, too restless to work on her Library of Congress notes, and gradually dozed in the velvet armchair Isabel kept at the window facing west. The sun, sinking by inches, warmed the sill at her fingertips. She smiled, despite impatiently awaiting her lover's return for dinner. Maybe if she focused, she could conjure Isabel that much faster.

Could one woman's desire speed the feet of her beloved? Could Hannah's breath blow wind behind Isabel's car, whisk autumn leaves into a flying carpet under wheels, float her lover through the bedroom window? *Come on, honey. I want you now. I want you now. I am haunted by you. I am haunted in your house. Come take me on this night of spirit chasing.*

Later, when the sun had disappeared and Halloween night proper began, lesbian ghosts and lesbian witches floated toward Sappho's Bar and Grill in the leafy light of dusk, the perfection of their assumed and practiced spookiness somewhat marred by the awkwardness of getting out of a Toyota in a flowing robe with a staff, or balancing a platter of vegan sugar skulls under an old sheet.

That night the bar talk turned again to favorite

library books, though now the participants were dressed as their historical avatars: Eleanor Roosevelt, Annie Oakley, Sojourner Truth, flappers, Arctic explorers, Disney princesses. The question they were nibbling on, along with beer nuts and chocolate stars, was a new one Hannah had posed: *Do you remember the first time you tried to find out information about gay people, at the library?*

"We-ell," began Kim, who originally hailed from Texas and was now costumed as a rodeo clown, "I was in my li'l cowgirl hat 'n' boots, cute as a rose, and my aunt Min caught me red-handed with my fingers in the H drawer of the card catalogue, trying to look up Homo. I thought just as fast as I could on my feet, and told her I was aiming to join the Four-H!" Everyone roared.

"I looked up the word 'tomboy,' because I was sick of being called that," said Trale, whose real name was not Trale and who enjoyed keeping everyone guessing. "Also looked up 'sissy' for my friend Frank. I liked my definition—he hated his. Then we looked up 'pervert.' That scared us. We never ate lunch together again after that, though it might have made more sense for us to fake being boyfriend-girlfriend, keep the talk at bay."

"I took out the book by Shere Hite—*The Hite Report,*" said Moira, who was about Hannah's age. "Talk about graphic! Whoa! But it didn't shout out gay, if you were pretending to check it out of the library as a research text. It was a national survey, supposedly of straight women."

This made Hannah remember one of her most ridiculous moments from early teenhood—or had she been twelve? Sipping one of Isabel's signature brews, the Witch Teat, she confessed, "There was a fairly progressive independent bookstore near us that had a big coffee-table volume on display one summer, *The Sex Book*. My best friend and I walked by it four or five times before she dared me to open it up to the pages with two women caressing. Then we fled, giggling, and hid behind a wall of comics to see how other customers reacted . . ."

". . . and she was probably holding your hand the whole time!" Yvette finished. "Me, I waited until my parents were away at their black fraternity-sorority reunion weekend, when we had our favorite baby-sitter, who let me do anything. I hightailed it to the library and took out *The Color Purple*. I wasn't allowed to see the movie so I knew there had to be something there. When I got to that line where Celie describes sleeping with Shug, 'It feel like heaven,' I was sold. Sold!"

"You know the publisher of Naiad Books, Barbara Grier—she said that when she was growing up she loved going into libraries and bookstores, flat-out asking if they had subject matter on homosexuality," marveled Dog. "And that was as a teenager in the 1950s! But it worked for her—that's how she met her first partner, a librarian, right? She thought she'd shock this lady by asking if the library had a copy of *The Well of Loneliness*. She got more than she bargained for in reply!"

"What about *The Happy Hooker?* That thing started with the writer seducing her childhood pal. Wasn't in any library I ever knew of, though. I found a beat-up copy of that when I inherited my granddaddy Bo's old Buick, and I learned a thing or two." Letty nodded, adjusting her Colonel Sanders outfit. "And I wasn't chicken to try, either. Haw! Haw . . ."

"Still trying—even if you're not exactly a spring chicken, now," Letty's partner teased.

"Oh! Oh! Women's *bookstores*," shouted Dog. "Where you could *buy* that shit. What about those?

They put those books right into our hands, and now they're vanishing like some freaking extinct *species.*"

"Not just the bookstores," Trale amended quietly. "We too are vanishing."

"Dog, I'm sure that various publishers, authors, librarians and bookshop managers themselves would be ever so thrilled to hear you reduce all of Amazonia to 'that shit,'" Carol observed. "But yes, that's an important piece of it. My life was saved by a women's bookstore. Thing is—you had to live in a city where there was one, have the nerve to enter it, and have a few precious lavender dollars to spend, too . . ."

"You didn't have to live *in* the city with a women's bookstore," argued Theodora. "I played both field hockey and lacrosse in college, and we were on the road all the time, sometimes for two-day conferences in other towns. All the dykes would sneak off to the women's bars after a game, but I'd get a lift to the feminist bookshop on my free hour."

"I drove for four hours in an ice storm to hear Mary Daly and get a signed copy of *Gyn/Ecology* . . ."

"I moved my ex-lover's fucking *piano* in exchange for borrowing her car to go to some mega-event at Sisterhood Bookstore when we lived in L.A . . ."

"I figured out the underground T system to get to New Words Books in Cambridge, but you needed a lift to go to Crone's Harvest, so I missed Lesléa Newman that time."

"Here's my question, Hannah," Carol called over the competing waves of memory. "How much time elapsed between that first sweaty encounter trying to check out a lesbian book at a library, and later realizing you could *own* the book via your local feminist bookshop?"

This deliciously inviting math problem silenced the entire bar. Isabel refilled drinks from her cauldron as nostalgic bookworms sipped, scribbled dates on wet bar napkins, and assessed the timelines of their own awakening. "So much candy for bookworms," smiled Isabel. The scent of smoky pumpkin spice wreathed their heads.

"Got it. I win!" roared Letty, signifying triumph with an earsplitting sneeze. "Took me sixteen damn years, you young ones, you baby dykes, you privileged little snots."

Dog hung her head. "Yeah. It was all in the same week for me."

"Three years," Hannah mused aloud. "Wow. I lived in the zip code for a great feminist bookstore, but I actually lacked the nerve. Can you believe that?"

"Of course we believe it. You went into a women's bookstore, you were announcing to the neighborhood, hello, I Am Queer." Moira sighed. "I dealt with that in Boston, and it wasn't pretty. Yeah, I got a black eye, pushed around by some punks in the neighborhood. Had to tell my mom I got the shiner bumping into a post. But I went back. I went back and I browsed in my Catholic schoolgirl uniform, underage in the erotica section, eating a saved peanut butter sandwich from my school satchel, dropping crumbs into that carpet, and they let me be. The woman's name was Jody. I called her Jody Putup because she put up with me every Saturday until I graduated from St. Ann's . . ."

"Wait. Here it is. Five years. We moved, just before Women and Children First Books opened, and it took me until college to live in another city with a lesbian bookstore . . ."

"I still haven't been to one. Because they're all gone, damn it."

"Not gone! I know one. Yvette, back me up on this, will you? Get over here."

"*Yeah,* gone, as in scarce, damn it." Yvette had her public relations notepad in her back pocket, obscured as usual by her spank-me scarf. "Look at this statistic. Mid-'90s, there were 140 feminist bookstores in America alone. And that was down by half ten years later. And today? We have, maybe, a dozen? Ten? What's up with that? Where are today's young ones going to go, to meet the rad poets and get signed copies of their manifesta?"

"Oh, gals, get global and look beyond the USA," Carol scolded. "There's a gay bookshop in London, one in Costa Rica, one in Paris, another in Barcelona, and one in Berlin, plus Savannah Bay in the Netherlands. And two in Australia and two in Canada. Don't forget those international lesbian archives. Isabel, aren't those some of the places you've been to?"

"Been to all of them, indeed, and beyond," was all Isabel would confirm, as she wrestled ghost-shaped cocktail umbrellas into a martini for Dora.

Hannah listened, head spinning pleasantly, as the regulars bantered and mocked one another, passed around snacks, danced, made out, and loudly criticized Congress. Her eyes wandered to the rare lesbian books Isabel had collected from trips abroad, shelved behind the bar in a beveled glass case about two feet wide. These books, at least, were safe from being lost, or forgotten, or given away, or shredded. Culled from both library sales and the best women's bookshops abroad, they were a signature fixture of Sappho's Bar and Grill.

One night last year Isabel had opened some of those books for Hannah and the characters had actually come out and danced with them.

No. No. She couldn't prove, ever, that this had ever happened. She had understood enough not to tell anyone about it. She hadn't even described it in her diary.

There was no record. No proof. But what if she cajoled Isabel into opening just one book, again? Maybe tonight? Now? In this atmosphere of Halloween magic, what might happen?

Her hand reached over. The hinged corner of the bookshelf was near enough to tap. Yes, the shiny door popped open. And to her horror, an early copy of Katherine Forrest's *Curious Wine* fell out, landing with a thump at Isabel's feet.

Her bartender lover turned, smiling but steely. "You spilled wine on the floor? I pour the drinks here. Come back here, my little bog myrtle. Come back here and pick it up."

"Uh-oh," someone cooed. "Hannah, you know Isabel's a keeper—don't mess with her collection!"

Did she mean Isabel's a keeper because she collects rare dyke books and won't throw them away? Or did she mean to warn me to pay attention to the relationship—that Isabel's the best partner I'll ever get, the one I better keep? Whose voice was that?

Confused, her ears pounding both from bending over to pick up the novel and the accumulation of several enhanced drinks, Hannah turned to look back at the sassing bar patrons. There was no one there. The barstools were, impossibly, empty all of a sudden. But on each seat lay the favorite lesbian book each woman had remembered from her journey into pride. As if on cue, the books flapped open to lie exposed and flat, split plummily, beckoning like paper vulvas. She was staring at them, just starting to say, "Wha . . .?" when the bookshelf behind the bar opened up like a dragon's mouth and swallowed her whole.

Chapter Four

Candy for Bookworms

She was behind the bar. Beneath the bar. In Isabel's secret wine cellar, the space she'd built herself and referred to obliquely as "the root cellar," so that no one but Hannah now knew it was a place for the really valuable and special vintages and liqueurs acquired across a lifetime (or times.) Racks of labeled bottles rose on either side of her, and the scent of dried juniper berries filled her nose. It *was* a true root cellar, too, after a fashion: knots of mushrooms and herbs askew on twine, sweet potatoes and potatoes for making vodka, and in the center of the very small room a carved wooden table where Isabel mixed ingredients or carefully decanted bottles. But on and around that table now were books.

They were the lesbian books of their rambling conversation, the ones she'd just glimpsed flopped open on her companions' barstools. Beloved early discoveries, well-thumbed novels, stolen and hidden stories by expatriate amazons of the interwar era in Paris. The books were perched upright on their spines, shifting and waving animatedly—and they were *talking. Laughing.* They were alive.

"She put me under her jacket, this pea jacket she always wore that year, and ran out of the drugstore," chortled one, a peeling volume of *That Kind of Love*. "Left her change on the counter, left her Coca-Cola, left her bike parked on its kickstand outside, and just ran! Later she had to come back for that Schwinn. She read me and read me all afternoon, all afternoon . . ."

"I had the girl who ate the sunflower seeds," mourned a pale copy of Colette's *Claudine* trilogy. "Those shells got into my spine and cut me. It was a whole s/m relationship—"

"Oh, you wish," snapped Colette's more explicit memoir, *The Pure and the Impure*. "You're just jealous because *my* readers were more likely to make love to themselves in front of me. I can't help it if not everyone found me before they got to college."

"I can name hundreds of girls who swooned and caressed when they read *Claudine Married!* Her whole affair with Rezi? Come on. You know it's true."

"Ah, to be caressed again!" sighed *You Are the Rain*. "Almost no one remembers me . . ."

"That woman tonight. She named you as her first."

"Yes, her first, her first!" crowed *Rain*. "I was somebody's first! Me!"

"Get over yourself. It is I they touch, touch, touch, looking for what is not theirs to have," said *The Well of Loneliness*, leather-bound and haughty. "I am assured of handling, of passing between women, between libraries."

"Will someone please shut her up?" demanded *Rubyfruit Jungle*. "There's about as much action in you to tickle a goat. I'm the one with the normal range of girlfriends—and survival. Hardly anyone comes out from a mansion, darlin'."

"You think you are so tough, my little American,"

sneered Tereska Torrès's *Women's Barracks*. "I have seen war. Caressing was a luxury for us."

Violette Leduc's *La Bâtarde* twirled provocatively. "I may not be explicit enough for some, too explicit for others, but for many I was *juuust* right. 'She was stroking the place where the buttocks touch. There were guitars quivering in my legs.' You can see where my binding is broken, where they only went to those pages. Ah, how the questioning adolescents love boarding school literature!"

The books *Olivia, Mädchen in Uniform,* and Madeleine L'Engle's rarely celebrated early work *Prelude,* all preened. L'Engle's later paperback *A House Like a Lotus* added, "I was pretty liberal for my time, wouldn't you say?"

"Liberal, yes, and sexless," complained *Even Cowgirls Get the Blues.*

"Oh, right. Like we need a book by a male author to be the authority here." The other books flared their pages. "I thought we agreed that one wouldn't be invited."

"Back off, separatists. This is Halloween: warlocks welcome as well as witches. Besides, this is about what the readers chose. Plenty of them chose me first! And face it: my pages have far more vagina-positive material and description than all of you combined. How many of *you* have the phrasing *folded labia, hooded clitorises, jaws aglisten, she smiled at your quiverings as she parted your asshole*? Top that. I can't help it if I came out of the swinging 1970s." Tom Robbins's *Cowgirls* had spoken.

"I had anal sex, if that's your litmus test," objected *Kinflicks.* "And my sex scene ended in 'a breathtaking series of multiple orgasms.' Do you know how many women wrote to my author? So there! Yes, I was important to many."

"Plus, I'm sorry, Cowgirl, but you're not a writer our readers could date," and Barbara Grier's *The Lesbian in Literature* was delighted to have the last word. "You're no lesbian role model, m'boy."

Hannah saw that the medical textbooks, scientific studies and surveys, and books like *Lesbian Love, The Grapevine, The Lesbian in Society* (all written by men) were self-segregated, smoking cigars together. "I still think it's dangerous, smoking so close to paper," complained *Patience and Sarah*. *The Price of Salt* replied, "Live a little, my dear."

It was impossible. Impossible. But the books were talking. They were reminiscing just as Hannah's friends had been reminiscing—about the first time someone loved them. About feeling loved, needed, important to someone. Inanimate objects, they were alive just for now, just this night, their spirits released by the nostalgic talk at the bar. They did not appear to notice Hannah, who stood motionless behind a post.

"But don't you feel," said Karla Jay's *After You're Out*, "kind of ripped off by the computer revolution? I hardly ever get touched now. They read me on their laptops, if at all. That's me, but not really me. Not like the early days when kids really felt up a paperback, jammed it in the back of a jeans pocket."

"To be held in the sweaty palms of a young woman coming of age was all I ever wanted," sighed *Beginning With O*, and *The Women of Brewster Place* shook her pages a little, and put in, "But we scared them."

We Too Are Drifting drifted over. "I have tea stains, avocado stains, jam stains, egg stains. Whoever owned me only read me at breakfast."

In Her Day began to sob. "I miss my bookworm. My bookworm," she wept.

And to Hannah's amazed eyes, each of the books

straightened her spine and shook, and from each fell a shower of snapshots. Old Kodak Brownie photographs with scalloped edges, Polaroid glossies, school poses in little wallet squares. They piled on the table, making a tower that eventually reached the cool cellar ceiling. These were stolen images of the girls who had most loved and treasured these books—read them over and over, scrawled notes in the margins with pencil, underlined passages in Bic pen or hot orange highlighter, had hidden the book from parents, babysitters, nosy aunts, bratty little sisters, housekeepers, anyone who might put their adolescent search in peril.

There were photos, too, of women well past college age, women who came out later in life and made the same trip to library or bookstore on older legs, on married legs, on legs that balanced a child in the curve of a mature hip. Such women had to hide their lesbian books from angry husbands, divorce lawyers, in-laws, sad-faced children. But these were readers who had an advantage of maturity. Already experienced in life, perhaps glib with pen or working in the editorial world, women coming out at midlife were often quick to make that leap from bookworm to author themselves.

Whatever each woman's journey had been, the books had been companion, witness, guide, instruction manual, warning light, welcome kit, oracle, miracle. Why wouldn't the books have loved, in turn, their owners, who reached for them with so much desperate hope when no other information was available, anywhere else? And if, somehow, late at night when the bookworms were sleeping, the books moved inch by inch to capture a school photo left on the edge of a desk, and absorbed it deep within thick pages . . . a keepsake of the owner . . . These, too, were relationships, love affairs, a meeting of minds that dispelled loneliness. This was a Halloween for books to conjure bookworms back to hold them once again.

Hold me. Hold me one more time. Wasn't I good to you? Didn't I help? Why'd you leave me? Please, just one more night. Hold me one more night. This night. Touch me. Gently . . .

And as the photos fluttered above the table and the books linked in a circle and howled for lost love, the wall behind Hannah shimmered again. She fell back into the bar.

But not the same bar. Sappho's Bar and Grill had become . . . *an ice cream parlor?*

Isabel's bar was now a way station for teenage dykes. On a long set of brightly padded stools that seemed to stretch toward infinity, schoolgirls and schoolgirl dropouts sat, each with a soda or milkshake or favorite snack of her own time, each with her nose in the best book of her own self-discovery. Isabel herself was there, not paying attention to Hannah yet, setting out root beer floats, Yoo-Hoo, ginger ale, Mountain Dew, moon pies, cherry and vanilla Cokes. Each girl took her treat without removing her eyes from the page she was reading. Several girls were simultaneously sipping their ice cream sodas and popping bubble gum. At different times, they each sighed and turned pages. A few were discreetly rocking their legs back and forth, thighs rubbing.

"Trick or treat," said Isabel, now noticing Hannah and smiling. Of a sudden the girls in front of them were their friends, the regulars at Sappho's Bar and Grill. Hannah saw Letty, Trale, Moira, Yvette, Shoni, Dog, Theodora and several others as they once were as teenagers—each wearing the clothes she might have worn, reading the book that changed her

84

life, drinking sweetness into her body, the body about to act on liking girls. Letty wore the blazer of a Louisiana parish vocational high school over pegged jeans, scuffed saddle shoes dangling; Yvette sported an Afro that filled the space around her head as she snacked from a bag of Funyuns; Dora was in her basketball uniform and early-model Adidas, drinking an Arby's Jamocha shake. In their hands were the books they had mentioned with such love: *The Color Purple, Rubyfruit Jungle, Sappho Was a Right-on Woman, Beebo Brinker.*

The books seemed to shiver with pleasure as they were held and paged over, like cats releasing deepest purrs, nearly melting into the hands that clutched them. She could see the connection between the reader and the read, the bookworm and the book, a silvery electric current sparking along the bar.

Then one young reader glanced up, just an instant's glance away from her book, and Hannah gasped. It was *her.* This was *Hannah* at sixteen, reading Ruth Falk's book *Women Loving* from the Intimate Book-shop. She had borrowed a multispeed bike she didn't know how to gearshift and lurched six miles from her high school to this bookstore to spend her birthday money on a book she knew was about lesbians.

There she was in her painter's pants and purple bandanna and Birkenstocks, wearing a mood ring and a woman's symbol necklace, drinking a coffee milk-shake (*I used to get those at Baskin-Robbins; this was years before there was a Starbucks anywhere . . .)* and reading about women who made love to other women. This was the last moment of innocence before everything began to happen. The last days of unformed consciousness.

Where were those painter's pants now? Had life

turned out the way Hannah expected? How many women had she learned to love? Would the number surprise her earlier teenage self?

"Whuh . . . hawchoo!" sneezed the teenage Letty, and all the other readers raised their heads and scolded, "Shhhhh!" The floating soda bar had all the sanctity of an archive. Brows furrowed (or raised) as readers came to particularly explicit or poignant pages. "No way," breathed Dog, sucking on a Jolt Cola, riveted by *Dykes to Watch Out For.* "*Shhhhhhhh!*" came from the girls on either side of her.

Then Isabel put her arms around the real and grown-up Hannah, and whispered in her ear, "Now look." And there was Isabel. *Isabel,* the barkeeper and mystic, whose past was never really fixed, but who evidently had one of her own. For she too was sitting at the bar for just an instant, a fifteen-year-old in a knit poncho and long skirt and hippie sandals, drinking herbal tea and absorbed in *A Woman Appeared to Me.*

Isabel looked up and looked at the older Isabel, and vanished with a puff of smoke. *Puff! Puff! Puff!* All of the girls were disappearing, only to be replaced by other girls—of every race and ethnicity and religion, of every nationality where LGBT books were still banned. Though the ice cream parlor barstools were soon overflowing with young women from Iran and Saudi Arabia and Yemen, there were girls from Brunei, Chechnya, the Congo, Zanzibar, North Korea. Their hands trembled as they opened the banned writings penned by lesbians, ancient or contemporary, from their own culture and language. Delicate foods replaced Western sodas and snack bags. The same silvery current of discovery and love surged afresh.

"This is the only place they can come to read,"

Isabel was explaining now. "And it's almost impossible to schedule, between Ramadan and all the other holidays. But a night or two here will keep these girls going for a year or more, until something changes. A revolution, a new education system, I don't know. I don't see that far ahead."

"Isabel." Hannah took a deep breath. "What is this place?"

And her lover smiled, and she too looked just a bit silvery and shimmering around the edges as she shrugged "Just another Overhead projection. But we'll need a Grand Reshelving, soon."

Then they were back at the bar. The real bar, Sappho's Bar and Grill, where the Halloween costume party was in full blast at half past twelve. Midnight had come and gone, and Hannah was holding two bottles of very old Welsh cider from the wine cellar, and wearing a dazed expression along with a cobweb.

Trale was on the dance floor, still a lithe tomboy at age eighty-six, swinging Moira round her back as strains of Madonna thudded. Yvette was break dancing as Dog hooted approval, and the pool tournament had ended with prizes of ghost-shaped cupcakes and Sappho's Bar T-shirts handed out to the winners. Several women had simply abandoned their cumbersome Halloween costumes and were dancing in bras and jeans, and then no bras, and then everyone had pulled off their tops and the dance floor bobbed with breasts.

I sure was born in the right time, thought Hannah, jumping up and down like a manic pogo stick in her circle of friends. *Literate. And loved.*

❦ ❦ ❦

The Halloween weekend continued to haunt her mind once Hannah was back in Washington, alone and unsure of her purpose. The crate of rescued books sat in her city apartment as the days ticked toward Thanksgiving. The dolly from the truck, stamped LIBRARY OF CONGRESS, was stashed in the closet underneath her now-unused academic robes. Sometimes Hannah thought she heard the books moaning in the night, or speaking to one another. She'd sit bolt upright, wondering if she had accidentally left the radio on, and the spooky cliterati murmurs would fade out. *It's just NPR, just NPR,* she told herself on those nights. But her radio button was always turned to "Off."

Isabel had spoken of a Grand Reshelving. In time, these books would be used for that purpose. In time. But as she washed her face, made her lunch, scuffed toward the Metro with her briefcase, dragged home at night and flipped on the evening news, Hannah heard that plaintive cry tingle right through her bones: "I miss my bookworm. My *bookworm.*"

As holiday decorations and shopping madness descended on Washington, Hannah did think of a new question to pose to her friends at the bar. She spent a short, sweet Thanksgiving weekend with her own family this year, her mother and aunts, her grinning nephews, charades and card games played in the den next to her old bedroom in the house where she had been young. *Before everything happened . . . grad school, teaching, women's bars, time travel.*

Hannah could hardly wait until the real luxury of her two-week Christmas break, which would bring her back to Sappho's in time for the solstice ritual Isabel always prepared.

Solstice Night served as a bridge across the complications of religion, and allowed everyone at the bar an opportunity to relax with chosen family—before some regulars drove over the river and through the woods to tense Christmas and Hanukah gatherings at homophobic homes.

Though it wasn't required, many women at the bar exchanged gifts and kisses at the frisky Solstice celebration, and everyone ate their weight in cookies and latkes. Best of all, Hannah was going back to Isabel, Isabel—those long lovemaking nights with Isabel that spun webs across place and space.

Hannah woke up on December 21 buried in the warmth of cranberry-hued flannel sheets, Isabel's arms around her waist. "Happy Solstice." Their knees and noses touched.

"Here's my little gift for you." Isabel handed Hannah a small, flat package wrapped in lavender tissue paper, flecked with gold. It was a signed first edition of Virginia Woolf's *A Room of One's Own*. "Where did you find this?" Hannah gasped, cupping it reverently between her palms, and hoping this book, at least, would sit on her shelf in silence. *Or is it meant to speak to me back in Washington?*

"Where did I find it? In England," Isabel demurred casually. "I do have a few connections there. And I know how you like Woolf. But I might become jealous."

In answer, Hannah straddled Isabel's left knee, then pulled a jewelry box from the pocket of the bathrobe she'd flung off rather late last night. "Check *this* out." She presented her lover with an unusual wristwatch she'd had designed in Washington: no numbers, no hands, but instead the four directions of a compass, with a tiny woman's symbol that ticked clockwise around North, East, South and West. As Isabel strapped it around her wrist, laughing in delight, snowflakes began to flutter against the windowpane. Yes, winter.

"Winter already—and yet I have so many months left in Washington," sighed Hannah. "You will wait for me, won't you? And if I never find another academic job, and just come back here and live with you and write, that would be all right?"

"That would be better than all right—although I can think of plenty of work we might both do, together, and not just at the bar." Isabel slid her long legs into striped winter tights. "Look. I thought I might be a candy cane, tonight. Will you help me shred potatoes and onions for latkes?"

"After kisses."

"Then kisses first."

"After backrubs."

"Oh, Hannah. Come here."

By 5 p.m. they had cooked and stirred and baked and fried and decorated, and the bar was packed with holiday revelers, some clad in characteristically revealing fancy dress. Letty, of course, played Santa, holding court at the back of the bar with one woman after another on her lap being interrogated with jolly scrutiny: "Have you been a good girl?"

Moira, dressed as an advent calendar, rotated around the room inviting women to open the cardboard-cutout doors taped over her breasts and remove chocolates. Dog was a queer elf, accompanied by Yvette, the Black Madonna. And assorted Hanukah Maccabees, solstice Wiccans and evergreen-bush ecofeminists clustered around the pool table, throwing back golden eggnog from the ornate shot glasses Isabel had set out.

Before the night grew too drunken, Cubby, the

young daughter of two regular members, played some holiday tunes and pagan rounds on her recorder, and Isabel sang a haunting medieval carol accompanied by Trale on lute. Then gift wrap flew and sheets of tissue paper skidded across the old wood floor as friends exchanged presents. The biggest surprise of the night came when Isabel unveiled her holiday gift to the community: an electric fireplace. "No more of that old gas heater that smelled like hell," marveled Carol.

During the first pause after gift-giving merriment, Hannah emerged from behind the softly burning Hanukah menorah to launch her survey. "What's the best or worst book anyone ever gave you as a present?" she asked. "Did anyone ever get a lesbian-themed book as a gift, maybe from your own family?"

Hoots of sarcasm greeted this idea. "Not bloody likely," Moira laughed. "I got the lives of saints." "I got a subscription to *Bride* magazine," added Yvette. "And a makeover."

"Why don't the people closest to us, who recognize the signs of our so-called 'lifestyle,' think to show their acceptance with a gift book?" Hannah probed. "Did any one of us ever dare to ask Santa for a dyke volume? Or would that request have made you unwelcome for the holidays?"

"I was already unwelcome," called out at least eight different voices. Some were very young voices. Hannah's former students. She reached out to touch Dez's hand for a moment.

But Yvette grew bold. "Hannah, I did ask my aunt, the one who never married, for a book by Audre Lorde, and she obliged. It came wrapped in silver paper, on Christmas when I was twenty-one and celebrating all alone in my first apartment."

91

"I liked *A Wrinkle in Time* and got a complete set of every book ever written by Madeline L'Engle, and guess what: there's lesbian characters in them there books!" chuckled Dog. "But you have to read all of them to get to *A House Like a Lotus*. Anyway, Hannah, the answer is yes: a book with a dyke character actually showed up under my Christmas tree because my folks hoped if I liked science fiction, I'd become a scientist."

"I got Nancy Drews, but I also got some other books about camping and scouting, and that led me to sleepaway Girl Scout camp and my first crushes," offered Hannah's graduate student Dez. "And skills from Girl Scout camp helped me at my first women's music festival . . ."

"What kinda skills we talkin', honey? Fire building or making out with older girls?" Letty wanted to know, pulling off her fake Santa beard to reveal her wispy actual beard. "They give any badges for *that*? This old butch would have made Eagle. Hand me one of them potato pancakes, kid."

Hannah had one final, very nervous question. "Anyone ever feel like a book wanted *you?*"

"Whoa," Shoni put in. "Yes. You mean, when the book chooses the owner? I've seen it happen. I've even seen books move across a table to get attention. The spirit world is powerful. And its medicine is very real here." She smiled at Isabel, who was suddenly busy washing shot glasses.

"It is real here. We all know that. This space is the best gift anyone ever gave me," said Trale. "This bar started as an escape for some of us, and turned into a homecoming." She raised her glass to Isabel. "Well, my dears, I'll say it. To the maker of magic, our solstice queen!"

And from behind the bar—very far behind the bar, where Hannah knew the secret cellar lay—there was the faintest sound of books sighing, an earthy fluttering that transcended every language but clearly was *Amen.*

The door blew open, and Winter came in.

Chapter Five

The Card Catalogue

After the holidays, when she was back in D.C., Hannah wasn't sure what to do. Removed again from Isabel and their community of boisterous bar dykes, she needed a good ear in the capital city. Were there any other federal Amazons open to talking about the supernatural?

She knew one: her counterpart at the Smithsonian, Efren, a handsome woman who handled some of the museum's own growing LGBT collection. Did Efren hear voices while trying to salvage and catalogue rare materials? On a snowy afternoon early in January, Hannah picked up her phone—the ordinary, land-line phone on her desk, though nothing felt ordinary any more—and called to see if her colleague might be free for a quick drink after work.

They met at Busboys and Poets, a center of black arts, spoken word, queer youth poetry slams and sumptuous soul food that paid homage to multiple cultures. "What I wanted to ask," Hannah yelled above the open mic going on in the Langston Room, "is if you ever get the sense that the objects themselves have feelings? Are more than inanimate? Does Eleanor Roosevelt's gown ever move around by itself after dark? Do you get spooked being in there alone with all that historic material?"

"Oh, you bet," was Efren's casual reply. "It's not just the gay ephemera, for sure. The kachinas we have definitely seem alive. I wouldn't spend a night in that storage cabinet with them; no way. And at least four people have reported seeing Julia Child cooking in that model of her original kitchen. I actually smelled duck a l'orange when I arrived early a few weeks ago, and let me tell you, that was no schoolkid's brown bag lunch left overnight. Haunting? Sure. Comes with the territory." Efren took a sip of her Foggy Bottom and looked at Hannah with bright blue eyes. "Are you having some close encounters, my friend?"

"I think just with the lesbian past," Hannah ventured, "although who knows. I think I'm meant to do something with a rare book collection that's been donated—maybe get it into the hands of girls who never had a lesbian book, acting fast before the era of digitalization changes the reading experience as we know it.

"Of course, I have such a personal relationship to this book collection. It more or less covers the whole of my own coming-out reading list. The donor has to be someone my age, maybe even someone I know; and that's another whole Scooby-Doo mystery. I know I'm here to do archive work but it feels so wasteful to have such books coldly warehoused off-site, out of sight, forgotten. And even if a lot of kids today can look up and order these books online from the safety and comfort of their damn mobile phones, that's not the same as encountering them in a real circulating library . . ."

"You mean like we had, where first you had to

negotiate a homophobic librarian who played cards with your parents or a dyke librarian who gave you that look along with the book. Face it, kid, times have changed. Young queers don't browse the library shelves for *After You're Out* or *Our Right to Love* or titles with the *L* word, like we did. The past is past. We archive it; we don't perpetuate it." Efren leaned forward. "But as long as we're sharing, it's the card catalogue that gets me."

Hannah felt her antennae go up. "Card catalogue?"

"Sure, the giant old one at your LOC before it was replaced by the modern system. When every researcher had to go and thumb through the old cards, then sign out a book with their real name. Now imagine the guts of the research babes in *that* era, who had to put a name on a federal card to get lesbian literature. I once worked on a project where I had to access that card catalogue and it blew my mind, the sweaty fingerprints on the corners of the most-requested books.

"I'm sure there were closeted scholars in the McCarthy era as well as actual agents looking at those books. When they checked out their choices, some researchers used obviously fake names—there are quite a few John Smiths and Mary Joneses, and in one hilarious case, a 'Miss Llangollen,' in homage to the eighteenth-century couple she was looking up.

"But there are also many borrowers whose names I recognize, who later became authors, politicians, activists, poets, professors like you." Hannah winced at this; she was no longer a professor, this year anyway. "Like you," Efren repeated firmly. "Anyway, it's a huge find, the signatures of the dead captured in this way, on their queer research pilgrimage."

Hannah's heart pounded. "If those cards could talk . . ."

"Oh, they do, they do," said the unflappable Efren. "And the atmosphere in that room where they're stored is an accumulated atmosphere, full of feeling. Panic, hope, discovery, triumph, fear. It's enough to knock you down. You work in that collection, you have to take a long cool shower afterward, the sweat of ages washing down your knees and into the Potomac.

"The Potomac River is full of museum DNA, by the way, since you're obviously interested in magic dust. Many were the museum staff secretly reading rare books in the bathroom while on break and then carefully washing their hands, sending tiny bits of book binding and ink down the drain and through the pipes." Hannah thought of the hours she herself had already spent in the Library of Congress bathroom. Why hadn't she thought of the haunted bathroom's sinks, carrying the dust of books into an underground river of memory? Did the *underground* complement the *Overhead*? Where did it all end up? Under the ocean? Back to Lesbos?

"Eat your corned beef on rye, will you?" Efren poked her. "Let me tell you about the objects that came in yesterday . . ."

Hannah couldn't sleep. Catalogue cards danced before her eyes, alive with names, fingerprints, the long-ago hunt for lesbian tribal history. What else might lie inside that fingerprint code? She grabbed her phone and dialed up the Snerd, her college roommate.

Snerd was short for "The Science Nerd," a nickname they'd bestowed on the only one of their friends to major in a STEM field; and the Snerd cheerfully conceded that it suited her better than her birth name,

Jade Wing. "That was a bird too weighted with precious stones to fly," she often joked.

Please, please, let her be working in her lab tonight, prayed Hannah, and to her relief the call was answered right away in typical Snerd style. "You? Now what?"

"Great to hear your voice, too. Look, I'm sorry to interrupt your research, but—"

"—but you have some sort of weird-ass lesbo problem only I can solve," the Snerd cut in. "Aren't there other straight women in lab coats right there in Washington, D.C. that you could bother at midnight? Why pick on me? You're not still in love with me, are you? I told you, I finally landed the nice Chinese boyfriend. My parents are ecstatic."

"Shut up. Listen. Could you, ah, hypothetically speaking, of course, but—is it possible to clone a person from sweaty fingerprints left on a library card?"

Long silence. Then: "I'm trying to win a grant just now, so I can't be involved in anything illegal. Just who are you trying to bring back to life?"

"Nobody! In particular . . . it's just an idea. What if there were dozens of fingerprints left on an object over time? Whose would be the dominant one?"

Hannah heard the snap of a soft-drink can tab being pulled as the Snerd settled back in her chair at the lab in Oakland. "Well, first of all, you're more likely to get DNA from something else one of your readers left, and it would depend on the card stock used at the time. You're talking about a library card? Wouldn't it just belong to one person at a time?"

"No, a card in the back of a book that you take out and sign in order to borrow the book. You remember. Dozens of borrowers would handle and sign it over time. And I'm also thinking about a card in a card catalogue that many hundreds of investigators touched, all trying to look up one specific topic. A topic like homosexuality, for instance."

Hannah could hear the gears turning in her friend's mind. "Well! I don't like the sound of this, but I'll tell you this much. It's very hard to build a genetic map from an ancient drop of sweat. But those cards could easily contain other body fluids and matter.

"How squeamish are you? So, in any group, you have bleeders and shedders. That means individuals who accidentally cut their finger on the item they're handling, let's say in your instance getting a paper cut from the card and leaving a bloodstain. Shedders leave a tiny grain of dandruff or spit. You'd be amazed how many adults put almost anything they handle in their mouths or against their lips. Just like babies! That's how epidemics spread."

All of a sudden Hannah remembered the line by Adrienne Rich, from her poem "The Photograph of the Unmade Bed." *A long strand of dark hair in the washbasin is innocent and yet such things have done harm.* That day in the Library of Congress bathroom when the phone rang and it was Adrienne Rich's voice, a long strand of dark hair had appeared on the sink and Hannah had rolled it in a paper towel and tucked it into her briefcase. Was it still there? She knocked over a partly filled wineglass to reach her bag. Yes!

"Jade, I have a strand of hair, too. It didn't exactly fall out of the card catalogue, but it's part of the mystery. Can I send it to you?"

"Hair! Now you're talking. You know DNA tests were done on a locket of hair from Mary Tudor in England, to help identify the old skeletons found in the Tower of London? Yes, hair testing is more my

100

area, so go ahead and send it, you nutball. But right now, I've got a test tube full of something I can't talk about, so are we done here?"

"I know, you have to get back to your experiment. Okay, thanks. Really," Hannah assured Dr. Wing. "Big love, Snerd, you're the best. And give my regards to the fiancé. He's one lucky dude."

"*His* relatives don't think so," said the Snerd, and hung up.

So maybe there are elements of women on those cards. Bloodstains? Why didn't I think of bloodstains? I get paper cuts all the time. It's a condition of the scholarly life . . .

Did she really want to try to reconstitute an army of ghosts? Wide awake now, Hannah sketched out possibilities in her journal. Maybe the strand of hair belonged to a woman of the past with something important to tell her. Maybe far back in the recesses of her confused brain Hannah had already considered this—cloning anew the best lesbian scholars of yester-year so that they'd be available for today's youth.

But that was a ridiculous idea. If what Efren had said was true, agents of the House Un-American Activities Committee would also have pawed through the card catalogue to find evidence against the radicals and liberals of the homophile movement. She'd be cloning from a spy's sweaty fingerprint DNA, too. The image of a J. Edgar Hoover lackey re-forming, spook-like, out of a petri dish in the Snerd's lab made Hannah release a distressed guffaw.

She was grateful to fall asleep laughing.

She dreamed of a river of book dust and human DNA. In her dream, all of the frightened scholars of the McCarthy era who went to the Library of Congress (and any other library, college, community) to find the limited info on gay and lesbian life were hiding in bathroom stalls, reading hungrily, taking notes, where no one could see. No one could see the titles on those books as they propped against anxious human thighs.

Afterward, almost as if the encounter with that literature had been actual sex, the readers washed their hands so carefully, so thoroughly, and after all, that action was a cover-up, too, for anyone who entered: *Me? Not reading! No, just came in to wash my hands, you see!*

Efren's conversation, and the Snerd's, tugged and filled the form around her dream. Little bits of paper, magic dust from every banned-book reading, washed into those sinks and to the river; sweat and human blood and drool and dandruff fell into the books, onto the book cards, catalogues. This was the great genetic swap meet of all time, the surface of the literature scraped off in minute wear over the years, replaced by the equivalent buildup of lesbian body effluvia.

There was no need to "clone" women of the past; they were *there*, now, built into the paper itself. Cards and book pages were so saturated with the essence of the reader that they became de facto extensions of the lesbian body. She tossed and turned, laughing in her sleep. No, she had not been sentimental or misguided in her feeling that there was something holy, alive, in treasured volumes that shouldn't be destroyed. Over time, books that had been loved acquired so much of each reader's DNA that the pages became living laboratories of women, women bound together . . . until recycled, or shredded.

And the same was happening *underground*, where, as Efren said, via the bathroom sink all the washed-away corners and dust of books met the washed palm sweat and loose hairs and papercut fingers of the reader. And under the Library, in the Potomac, all that human longing for the right book was somehow reconstituted . . . but reconstituted as what? What came out of the underground waters? Who were the mystical beings made up of knowledge and female essence?

Naiads, of course. The original bookworms.

But who was the weaver below, who plucked all those elements from the drains and formed the naiads? Sorting Library flow from other garbage—leaving out the stubs of ball games, flushed-out tissues, watered grasses from the White House lawn, rain spill, day camp apple juice, snowflakes, bike oil, bakery oil dribbles from Georgetown Cupcake? Who siphoned and panned and strained the lesbian bits and book dust?

A worthy counterpart to the Overhead would be the Underbrewster. She who stirred a witches' brew of naiad juice. Some fabulous mixologist . . .

No. No.

Mixologist?

Bartender.

It couldn't be . . . Isabel?

Her lover was the Underbrewster.

When Hannah woke, her eyelids flickered just briefly over the enormous possibility that her now long-distance partner might be the goddess of book juice.

But she pushed aside the dream and went to work. There was plenty to do. She had her day job. Keeping up with ordinary archival work protected her right to roam around conjuring plans to relocate books. More and more, she was beginning to feel like a spy, planted by the Overhead, of course, but differently purposed than her very decent and caring colleagues in the Library.

Or was she? It occurred to her that *every* librarian and archivist might belong to a secret sisterhood none of them could articulate out loud. *Every* coworker she passed in the corridors, men as well as women in laminated ID badges and forearm-rolled sweaters, might in fact be on a mission from above, all sternly and lovingly engaged in the business of preserving what had been marginalized to the point of scarcity: black literature, lesbian literature, banned and beloved memoirs. Perhaps others were also outraged that duplicate copies of "their" books had been targeted for shredding.

There came a day when Hannah was in the bathroom and it occurred to her that she hadn't had her period in five or six months. *This isn't perimenopause any more,* she thought with a strange pang of regret. *I am entering actual menopause. Goddess knows, I am certainly not pregnant.*

She studied herself in the mirror while older and younger women moved busily around her, hastening to rejoin their tour groups or workdays. So, this was aging. Some gray hair, not much. A few wrinkles. Definitely more facial hair than before—but what counted as "before"?

She had always identified fully with whatever age she was at the moment: kid, adolescent, underage baby dyke, grad student, middle-aged scholarly warrior. Isabel loved her now, and touched her aging features with wise and affectionate hands: that should be all that mattered. How did the menstrual cycle even connect to vanity? Why had she gone from thinking about her disappearing periods to wondering if her face would disappear? How much had she bought into the beauty myth? What sort of feminist was she? Where were her overalls and bandanna, now that she worked for—oh, no—the *government?*

As if to underscore this point, the twenty-two-year-old woman next to her at the bathroom mirror carefully applied a gloss of blood-red lipstick, straightened her tightly clinging yoga pants and sashayed out, leaving Hannah alone in the room. Oh my god, thought Hannah forlornly, I'm a hundred and two.

At that minute, the phone rang.

She ran for it, grateful no one else was around. The phone felt sticky. There was almost a sensation of the ringtone throbbing right into her lower belly. And then a rich, thick current of a voice chuckled into her ear: "Missing me already?"

It sure wasn't Isabel—or her mother. "Who is this?" gasped Hannah.

"This is your menstrual cycle calling you to say goodbye. It's been a great thirty-eight years, but I'm done and you're free. I left the keys on the sink and you don't owe me anything, though you might have had a baby, you know, and maybe given me a year off. This whole deal with lesbians is just bewildering, I must say. Any last questions, before I head out?"

Hannah had hundreds of questions, but couldn't find her voice. Her cycle? Goodbye? What keys? How could her period *talk?*

"Sorry for any hurt I've caused," her period sang. "You always hurt the one you love . . . Did I ever mention my favorite punk band is The Cramps? Say, did you hear the one about the four little kids who don't have enough money between them for a Saturday outing, and then they decide to pool their two dollars and buy a box of tampons, because the box says if you use tampons you can go skateboarding, waterskiing, swimming . . ."

Hannah's period, it seemed, also moonlighted as a stand-up comedian. "I have plenty to ask you if you'll shut up for a moment," she shot back. "For instance, what did women do about their periods while living as nuns in the ninth century, or while traveling by covered wagon, or while passing as men in the mines?"

"Sorry, gotta go," sang the menstrual caller. "I'm cycling out. It's been real. Use the keys! My friends will talk. Shalom! Eve sends her regards." There followed a rude remark in ancient Hebrew, and then the line went dead.

Hannah stood in the bathroom, unsure what had just happened. One thing was clear: she was unlikely to get her period ever again. Celebrate, or lament? What to do with all those tampons at home? Donate them to a women's shelter? Bury them and have a mock funeral? No more monthly cravings for chocolate and salt. Actually, she had those cravings every day now. Middle age and menopause were a constant diet struggle.

Before she could move away from the phone, the bathroom door swung open and three nuns entered, Senate visitors' passes clipped to soft blue habits. Hannah watched in embarrassment as the youngest of the three reached up calmly to place a coin in the sanitary napkin dispenser. Here was her answer: nuns were like every other woman, making do with whatever materials were available in their era, reminded each month of the possibility of motherhood they chose not to fulfill. Like so many lesbians, thought Hannah. The different path. But a woman all the same. Then she saw the keys.

"Are those your keys?" asked the eldest nun. "Don't forget your keys." She held out a set of small, shiny brass keys on a ring with a fob that said RED SEA. "Oh! Were you recently touring the Holy Land?"

"Ah, no, Sister," replied Hannah, thinking fast. "The

106

Red Sea is an Ethiopian restaurant in the Adams Morgan neighborhood."

"We ate there last year during the Catholic University symposium," yelled the third nun from behind a stall. "When Sister Dorothy got her library science degree."

Hannah took the keys, and then stopped in her tracks. There was a lock on the sanitary napkin/tampon dispenser, right at eye level on the wall. Someone must come in every so often, unlock the box and refill it. But perhaps the lock would reveal something else. Yes, it was exactly the right shape to fit the brass key in her fist. She'd have to come back later. Much later, when absolutely no one would walk in.

This wasn't the first time that Hannah had stayed after work and hidden until everyone but the security guards had departed. The question was whether sneaking into the women's bathroom would set off an alarm. She had prudently wedged the bathroom door open with a wadded paper towel hours earlier, in case there was an automatic lock set to some sort of after-hours timer. She settled into the womblike space beneath her office desk with a banana, a granola bar, and a copy of Lillian Faderman's *To Believe in Women*. At 9 p.m. she emerged from her hiding post and entered the women's room, keys in hand.

The pay phone regarded her silently. It did not ring or even chirp as, trembling, Hannah fit the first stout little key into the tampon dispenser. All of a sudden she thought of Pandora's box, the ancient Greek myth. Just what might she be unleashing? Or there might be nothing at all inside. She'd feel like a fool, wasting an uncomfortable evening on a prank . . . a prank call made by whom, exactly?

Suddenly, with a trill of tropical birds, winged sanitary napkins burst out of the wall dispenser and began flying around the room like swifts, calling to one another. "Whee!" "Yippee!" "Yahooo!" One rode the air in surfer motions, curling into the shape of a Dewey Weber longboard, howling "Cowabunga!"

They flapped enthusiastically around Hannah. "Much obliged, sister!" "We never get out." "Stay free! Stay freeeee!" Linking up, the winged pads formed a sort of circle, bobbing and dancing. "And now you get three wishes! Think wisely. But we know what you want!"

Three wishes? Once liberated, the flying pads turned into genies? How could they know what Hannah wanted? She batted at this battalion of cotton batting. "What am I supposed to ask for?"

On command, the napkins rearranged to form the shape of a mountain Hannah recognized at once. It was Half Dome in Yosemite National Park.

Half Dome! Was it the summer between her junior and senior years of high school, when Hannah's dad had taken her to Yosemite for the climbing trip they'd planned and looked forward to forever? And on the morning of the excursion, she'd awakened with excruciating cramps and heavy bleeding, unable to move. The park ranger shook his head, warning that any malevolent grizzly bear could scent her now, and the whole outing had been canceled. *It's because I'm a girl,* Hannah had wept. *Why am I being punished? Being born female really* is *a curse!*

Now these flying menstrual fairies had her number. "One, two, three!" they chorused, and Hannah found herself in sturdy mountain boots, perched on the summit of Half Dome with her father, hale and hearty in his best year, the two of them munching raisins and peanuts from a plastic bag while joyfully overlooking what Ansel Adams had called "the range of light." Below their swinging boots lay all of Yosemite Valley, clad in gold, clouds and cliffs lit up with sunset glow, and the scent of campfire and pine needle and redwood achingly remembered. She was here. Here, with Dad, triumphant, an ascending Amazon, delivered into the view she had longed for, dusty hiker-climber scratches on her legs. And her legs were those of a seventeen-year-old feminist, unshaven as they had been. And, as ever, her father was shaking his head in amusement over that choice of not shaving, saying to her, as he once did, "When we get home, remind me to loan you the lawnmower."

Yes. That's exactly what he said. But look at us. Look at me. I scaled Half Dome! And indeed, other hikers were coming over to congratulate them, in the kinship fashion of climbers, and almost none were women. Just Hannah. But no: there was one female couple, dressed alike in battered windbreakers. And they looked at Hannah with the recognition that passes between women who love women, and smiled.

Oh! Yes, that was my second wish, when I was seventeen. Would I ever meet a real lesbian? And how would I know? Would I ever see a real lesbian couple, two women who held hands in public not caring what anyone thought of their love? I did meet a lesbian couple at Yosemite that year. They did smile at me in recognition. They did hold hands on the trail. I never knew their names, or how to thank them.

"Our names are Barb and Nancy," said the couple, fading now to sunset mist. "We knew you, and we knew you knew us. Take care, sister . . ."

Then Hannah was back in the bathroom and no one was there. The box on the wall was closed and locked. No mini-pads flew around the quiet tile, no keys were gripped in Hannah's shaking hand. There was nothing to show what had just happened. She felt a wave of bitter disappointment that her father was gone and her period was gone, and she was no longer a daughter and had not become a mother. She wanted to be young again and climb alongside her father, who loved mountains. Her life now was so sedentary, and Yosemite was on the opposite coast from D.C., and were her hiking years behind her? Maybe so.

But curiously, she seemed to have some scrapes along her legs, some pine needles in her socks. And her legs felt soft with hair left growing wild, although surely she had shaved her calves last night?

The phone rang. And it was a very ordinary voice, the voice of Hannah's photo lab developer from her drugstore at Dupont Circle, merely saying, "Your portrait is ready." When she hung up the phone, she saw in the keypad's shiny metal reflection that something had been placed on the bathroom sink. It was a framed photograph of Hannah and her father, legs swinging over the precipice atop Half Dome, signed in her father's neat handwriting, *Wish you were here.* In the background, hiking downward, were two women holding hands.

Wish number three. I just wanted proof he was thinking of me. Hannah rushed gladly toward the picture, only to have it fade and then vanish altogether in the four seconds it took to cross from pay phone to sink. The portrait was gone. There was no proof.

Steps in the hallway outside reminded her that at this late hour she was trespassing illegally and had better skedaddle. The security guard was approaching.

She stood absolutely still for a long moment, and then tiptoed out of the bathroom and out the side exit she had propped open earlier. The Metro was still

110

running, and she joined other late-working Washing-tonians wearily peeling off Capitol Hill and outward toward suburbs. The usual single-tracking delay gave her a few extra moments to wonder what had just happened.

There's a connection—first bleeding, last cycle, woman-hood, paper. I raged against my period for keeping me from hiking. But we who came of age with second-wave feminism were radically essentialist, hiding under the covers with copies of Our Bodies, Ourselves, *looking at the diagrams of our own vaginas, writing in our diaries about the drama of our first periods . . .*

That was it! Suddenly Hannah remembered her dream from weeks before, inspired by the conversation with her friend Efren: the vision of an underground river made up of book dust and women's handwashing. In that river she saw the ashes of burnt diaries, girls' thrown-away diaries, the embarrassed, destroyed truth-telling of generations. That, too, was a literature flushed away, hidden and yet shimmering with life. Those ashes mingled with other book dust. Hannah had saved her own journals, but too many other young women had been terrified of discovery, of being outed if their diaries were found. This was a lost genre flooding global waterways, tiny bits of paper, badly burned school pads, shredded confessions. How much magic lay in those tender pyres? Where did it all end up?

Am I supposed to reconstitute all the lost lesbian diaries of the world? Return them to their original owners? Crawl into the sewers of D.C. and catch the pages being burned as they're flushed down? Oh, no. Not that. Surely not that. Please, Sappho!

She buried her head in her arms.

🐏 🐏 🐏

Later, at home, she threw off her clothes, grabbed a cookie and called Isabel. "So let's say Sappho's poems were burned by angry Christians offended by her desire for other women," Hannah began.

"That's one way to start a late-night erotica call," laughed Isabel. "Good to hear your voice, too, my darling!"

"I know. I'm a failure at phone sex. There's too much on my mind. But honestly, did you ever think about where those ashes ended up? Suppose not all her work was burned completely and some fragments could be reconstituted into poems?"

"That is what happened. That's how we have some of her surviving work today. You know that."

"Yes, but . . ." Hannah struggled to sound coherent. "If the ashes wound up in the rivers where ordinary women dipped their water pails, that means that generations of Greek and Roman and Turkish girls were . . ."

". . . drinking Sappho," Isabel finished.

Hannah paused. "And in this country, we're still drinking from rivers and waters that contain writings burned by women. Or even women burned as witches . . ."

"Go on. Puzzle it out."

"We are Sappho!" Hannah shouted, never minding a sleepy bang on the wall from her neighbor in the adjoining apartment. "We *are* the witches. We are the books. We are formed from the women in the water. We are the naiads!"

And far away in the distant city that had been home, where her lover the mystic still lived and ran the bar, she heard the joyous chuckle erupt from Isabel's throat, so loving and yet terrifying with power. And Isabel whispered, sounding so close by, "Hannah, I am the mixologist to your Overheard. What do you think a lesbian bar really is? A place where we reconstitute ourselves, across time, as all the women who have ever been challenged and survived. And we drink to those women, and we drink of those women, and we continue in every generation as those women. Their lost words, their essence. Do you understand, now, that this is the essence I've been mixing into those drinks? It is the essence of every lesbian across time that I have stockpiled in my wine cellar."

Chapter Six

A Reception for the Banned

"Someone must have come by while you were at lunch," said Aurora. "They left what looks like an invitation on your desk. Well, I'm off. Cheers!"

Hannah waited until she was certain she was alone—the other staff were at a budget crisis meeting—and then, glancing into the hall to be sure of no impending interruption, sat down at her desk. The invitation had her name embossed with a soft green type the likes of which was not used in her time, and seemed to be a card scroll tied in a fabric ribbon. The ribbon had clearly once been used for some other purpose, with a single long white hair clinging to its frayed fabric. Whose hair? An invitation from whom? From where?

She unrolled it. The elegant handwriting *(Whose handwriting? Whose ink?)* was a summons. It read, *Miss Hannah Stern is requested at the Reception for the Banned.*

That was it. No time, place, date. But wait—even smaller letters added, *RSVP.* How was she supposed to respond?

She found herself heading to the women's bathroom on the ground floor. It would be very crowded at this hour. There'd be docents, tourists, school field trips and church youth groups, library staff reapplying lipstick after lunch, security guards on break. It was risky. But she had to make an attempt. It wouldn't look odd anyway, to anyone paying attention, if she went to the pay phone and dialed for information. Would it?

Luckily for Hannah, there were only three women in the lounge when she entered, all washing their hands and laughing about a previous night's TV episode. She hesitated, then picked up the pay phone receiver and fumbled in her pocket for quarters, not sure what number to dial. She needn't have bothered. Before she had even attempted to deposit a coin, there was a voice on the line, distant and watery, intoning one word: "Go."

"Um, hello," Hannah sputtered, and then collected herself. "If I am speaking to the right party, I just got your . . . invitation. Where is this . . . reception?"

Silence. Whooshing like an ocean wave, which grew, and swelled, and passed. Then: "We're dining up there, now. *Won't* you come and see us? We'll be waiting." The line quieted to silence. Then the loud blare of a phone left off the hook.

Up there! Was this a summons from She, the Overhead? No, this had to be something else. Some sort of library mystery occasion. Hannah returned the phone to its holder and backed away. Now, dining "up there." There was in fact a dining area, a café, on the top floor. It would be closed for the after-lunch cleanup, wouldn't it? And thus used for some other purpose without much notice. What about the kitchen workers, though? Were they possibly in on this "reception"? She headed to the elevator on wobbly legs. Then, as she rode up to the top floor, it occurred to Hannah to take out her hairbrush and sweep it over her head, to tug her blazer into place, pull up her socks. When summoned by unknown entities to a party, it was always good to look your best.

She felt something strange but recognizable transforming her posture as she rode up one more floor: her hips, legs and shoulders were shifting into what the photographer Joan Biren had called in her lesbian slide show, "the look, the stance." She was standing with one hand on her hip and one eyebrow up when the elevator opened, presenting not just as a scholar but also as a dyke.

The cafeteria had vanished. Hannah found she was in the foyer of a richly tapestried restaurant. At the entrance, holding a golden clipboard, stood a small gray-haired figure she recognized—a writer she'd met and corresponded with, and who had only recently passed away: Nancy Gardner, author of the young adult novel *Annie on My Mind*. "You got your invitation!" said Nancy, gliding toward her on sneakers that hovered just about half an inch above the gleaming hardwood floor. "This way." She pulled aside a beaded curtain, and a roar of conversation and tinkling glassware greeted them, along with delicious smells. Poached fishes, roasted potatoes, partridges in sauce, wines, rosewater puddings . . . egg creams? *Wait a minute. This menu comes from some of my favorite books!*

"'The lunch on this occasion began with soles, sunk in a deep dish, over which the college cook had spread a counterpane of the whitest cream, save that it was branded here and there with brown spots like the spots on the flanks of a doe,'" Virginia Woolf quoted herself as she floated toward Hannah.

"Why on earth would they ban us when we mostly

wrote about food?" demanded Gertrude Stein. "They fear our sensuality, the power of the senses to arouse." She handed Hannah a glass of absinthe. "And this was banned as well, after our time." She sighed.

"Because it had elements certain to trigger madness in the soul," explained Renée Vivien. "I should know. I stopped eating and only drank absinthe."

Hannah looked around. A Reception for the Banned. These were the women whose books had been banned, censored, excoriated by shocked critics, denounced at public trials by pompous judges, hounded from the shelves of libraries, criticized at PTA meetings and school board hearings, in newspaper reviews and editorials, from the pulpit, in evangelical literature, in the Catholic List. Regardless of the quality of their writing, which ranged from admittedly awful to superbly crafted, these women had borne the sting of rejection simply due to subject matter—and because of who they were. Not all at this gathering were gay. But all were women of their time in ways that had shocked and prodded and opened up society. Independent women, intellectual women, lesbian women, feminists, bluestockings . . .

"Oh, there were plenty of other words to describe us," said Gertrude Stein, and Radclyffe Hall added: "I am indeed a congenital invert, myself." Hall quoted from James Douglas, the editor of the *Sunday Express*: 'I would rather give a healthy girl or boy a phial of prussic acid than this novel.' Really!"

"You could be swept off the shelf no matter how many prizes you'd accumulated if parents disliked your tone," snapped a woman with short hair and a Southern accent, and Hannah stood with head bowed before her favorite children's book author, Louise Fitzhugh. "Parents objected to my *Harriet the Spy* because she described people in her notebook. She seemed to operate independently of adult authority. Well, welcome to the twentieth century!"

"That was the only children's book I ever had where the main character wanted to be a writer," Hannah said. "And it took me years of research to confirm that you were gay."

Fitzhugh shrugged. "Most of the kids who wrote me said their favorite characters were Harriet, and Scout in *To Kill a Mockingbird.*" She jabbed a thumb in the direction of a little woman eating a slice of cake. "Nelle still won't cop to being lesbian, though it's always been so obvious to the rest of us. But no question about her being invited to the reception: *Mockingbird* was banned, and banned, and banned again."

In this stellar crowd of ghostly stars of literature, all of whom had felt the sting of rejection by both family and censors, waitresses circulated with elegant trays of every food lovingly described in all the authors' books. Women stood in threes and fours, graciously nodding to the ghostly waitstaff, accepting aperitifs and hors d'oeuvres, laughing and flirting, the living and the dead: Jane Rule, Maya Angelou, Radclyffe Hall. Judy Blume, Alison Bechdel, Madeleine L'Engle. Alice Walker, Lesléa Newman, Lillian Hellman. A large glass-topped centerpiece, set up amid thirteen linen-covered tables, displayed yellowed newspaper clips and journal pages detailing the banning or removal of each woman's book. Fascinated, Hannah turned toward this exhibit, much of which was very familiar to her from the American Library Association's "Banned Books Week" project. During the 1990s, some of the most frequently banned books included *Heather Has Two Mommies, The Color Purple, Annie on My Mind,* and almost everything by Judy Blume. Also in the display were several copies of the lesbian magazine *Bad Attitude.*

"That last one's mine," said a woman Hannah didn't recognize. "Were you part of the sex wars, sister?"

"I—no," stammered Hannah, remembering too late that this was a political term for the standoff between pro- and anti-pornography feminists in the 1980s. Women Against Pornography and the Feminist Anti-Censorship Task Force had spent bitter years WAP-ing each other in the FACT. But no, it had not been funny. At all.

"Yep," affirmed the woman, who wrote erotica. "You know that women like Andrea Dworkin and Catharine MacKinnon worked to pass anti-pornography statutes in major American cities and even joined forces with some right-wing groups to ban porn as harmful to women. Well, Canada paid attention. In 1992 my Canadian Supreme Court declared that even 'sex without violence that is degrading and dehumanizing' toward women could be banned. And within six weeks the Toronto cops seized this magazine from our women's bookstore and arrested the manager, who happened to be a woman I loved, and then what? Then what?" A sturdy team of Canadian lesbian ghosts, all in ice hockey goalie shirts and holding double-double coffees in Tim Horton's cups rather than champagne, now surrounded Hannah. It hadn't occurred to her that *Canadian* ghosts could be threatening rather than friendly.

"You took away our erotica," these spirits moaned.

"The Ontario court allowed for censoring all lesbian literature and held it at the border. Said that lesbian love, like gay love, was 'devoid of any real, meaningful human relationship.' Anyone who mailed us books had their shipment seized, and the bookshop owners were all charged with obscenity. What a loss for our readers!"

"But you fought it in the courts," Hannah recalled.

"Till we ran out of money. Did you ever know any feminist bookstore owners with bottomless pockets? These are some of the reasons those bookstores went out of business. And you did that! You American feminists!"

"It wasn't me!" Hannah cried. "I, I only went to one anti-porn rally! It was in opposition to that image of a woman in a meat grinder! I never meant for love stories to be confiscated at the border!"

"Yes, welcome to the reception for the banned," and ghostly bookshop managers in maple leaf jackets swarmed over Hannah's body like angry bees. "It begins any time just one woman's writing is banned. More writing gets banned than anyone planned. Understand?"

"She gets it. Leave her be." It was, again, Radclyffe Hall, the writer Hannah had "met" once before in a ghostly birthday encounter. Hall and Virginia Woolf regarded one another over Hannah's head. "Hullo, John," murmured Woolf.

"I was banned." Hall stood in the center of the room, brandishing the stem of her champagne glass. "I was defended by Vera Brittain, you know, the author of *Testament of Youth*. She told the press, 'Persecution and disgusted ostracism have never saved any difficulty in the world.' Yes, and despite her support—and Vita's," she gazed at Woolf again, taking her measure, "I was taken to court, on trial for *obscenity*, mind, starting on November 9, 1928."

"And I can't for the life of me see how," jeered Fitzhugh. "Where *is* the obscenity in that novel? Where are the hot parts? The whole book rambles toward that one line, 'and that night they were not divided.'"

"Naw—there's infidelity in there. And adultery. 'Took her and kissed her on the lips, as a lover.' That

121

line caused trouble; but didn't that line warm up your cave? It did mine," said Dorothy Allison.

Hall looked pained to have her magnum opus debated as arousing or not. She pulled from a waist-coat pocket her notes on writing *The Well of Loneliness* and quoted herself. 'What happened in England was a Government prosecution, two Police court actions both of which we lost in truly amazing circumstances, and as a result the suppression of the book which, however, was published again in Paris unabridged and in its original language within one month of that suppression. Had I required proof of the blind and bitter antagonism that exists against the inverted, and which in itself shows the vital necessity that existed for the writing of my book, then I had that proof as I sat in the police courts and listened . . .'

Margaret Sanger interrupted. "Yes, we know. But consider what I went through! My birth control advocacy, printed in my magazine *The Woman Rebel,* was duly seized by U.S. postal authorities and banned as obscene well before the Great War, oh so many years before your Canadian debacle. I had to leave the country and take up residence in Holland. And when I returned, arrested again! I went on hunger strike, only to be force-fed. My sister Ethel and I . . ."

Woolf, who had defended Hall in England, pointed out, "But, dear Margaret, recall that the New York police also invaded the office of Hall's American publisher and confiscated 865 copies of *Well of Loneliness.* We have, so many of us, tasted humiliation."

"I prevailed," boomed Hall. "Oh, you Americans, for whom I have such gratitude! American law, yes, federal law of 1929, held up literary merit as evidence! Literary merit prevailed! I was found to deal with 'a delicate social problem' and all charges were dropped!"

"I don't know about her *literary merit,*" whispered Woolf to Vita Sackille-West.

"I heard that," snapped Hall.

"But then why would you go backward in time to those repressive 1920s by setting up a climate for banning dyke lit in Canada?" the contributor to *Bad Attitude* challenged Andrea Dworkin, who had materialized in full battle dress—her beloved denim overalls.

And pointing to Radclyffe Hall, she said: "You're no better. You looked down on the lower classes and the working class women who wrote steamier scenes than you dared. You preferred, and I quote, 'The worthy among the inverted—those fine men and women whom Nature has seen fit to set apart as variants from the more usual type. . . . I do feel very sad when I read some of the books that have rushed through the door over my dead body, books giving a completely distorted idea of true congenital sexual inversion . . . worse still, books written with an eye to sales, dirty, unworthy, lewd little books . . . stressing only the physical side and thus throwing the whole picture out of drawing.'"

"You use my defense against me?" cried Hall, and Dorothy Allison quickly put a hand on the handsome Canadian: "Whoa, big fella. Let's chill." The hockey team hissed.

All of a sudden Hannah found her tongue. "Look, I don't support book banning. I did once get a billboard taken down that had an offensive message, but I'm—I'm here to get maximum distribution." Feeling drunk from the party punch, she liked the sound of what she'd just said. "Maximum distribution!"

Nancy Gardner glided over and rang a small silver bell. "Please, no more bickering. This is a reception. All are received here. And we will honor all those who never had the books we wrote for them, due to any cause—censorship, book banning, obscenity trials, seizure, confiscation . . ."

"Poverty, racism," added Jewell Gomez. "Illiteracy, segregation, violence."

"Religion." "Fire." "Sexism." Hearing these words, Hannah immediately thought of Passover seders at Sappho's Bar and Grill, where barriers to freedom and fulfillment were similarly named as the real ten plagues for women and for lesbians in particular.

And after the moment of silence, one beautifully dressed and buxom librarian ghost shimmered into view, and said in a breath of printer ink and leather-bound pages, "Let us remember together: we are in a library, a very good public library; and the point of the public library is to give the people what they want. We, too, all of us, want a book to fulfill its highest mission, which occurs when someone reads it. It is not decorative, nor a proponent of its own contents; the book itself is not responsible for imparting knowledge—that is indeed the author's lookout, yes. But a book without a reader is a wretched object. And a reader without a book, likewise desolate. Let us pledge anew to mitigate against such desolation."

They clinked their glasses, the living and the dead.

"And look you to the gallery," said Woolf. At the window, which in ordinary time opened to the hall-way beyond the Library dining café, faces of eager girls pressed against the glass. But in spite of their obvious excited impatience, they left no breath marks.

"They are the readers waiting for our banned books to be freed," explained Nancy Gardner. "They await the Grand Reshelving, as you see. We're all depending on you, you know, young Dr. Stern, to get those books to them."

Hannah gulped. And with that, the reception disappeared like vapor, and she was standing in the middle of the upstairs cafeteria, holding a cheeseburger she didn't recall ordering, surrounded by the usual bustle of cafeteria workers cleaning up from lunch.

That night, at home on her temporary but now familiar D.C. apartment sofa bed, Hannah pawed restlessly through the pages of banned book titles she'd assembled after the mysterious "reception." It had been *real,* the food, if not the ghosts, for an errant sesame seed was still under her fingernail. Could she send it to the Snerd? The drinks had been exotic, but at least one had tasted like Isabel's special brew. What was the recipe for what her beloved mixologist provided, across time? Could she ever ask? Would that end the parade of sweet sublingual experiences if she did? Sighing, she turned off the bedside lamp and let the lingering question of censorship fill her thoughtful darkness.

Who were the *women* who had banned women's writing? It was all well and good to blame The Patriarchy, but any number of women in every era supported the powerful men of their time, thus securing power and status for themselves. Old, old story. Women terrified of being accused of witchcraft fired an opening salvo of blame at a hook-nosed neighbor, or someone who had missed church once.

She had known such bristling PTA moms herself back in the mid-1970s, in junior high. In fact, if Hannah cared to remember—cared to reexamine that painful time of her own powerlessness, in ninth grade—she'd have to admit that her first encounter with a book-banning mom was also her first experience with homophobia: a PTA grown-up who called her out for loving her best friend *that way*. Jordan Matthews's mom.

Whoa! That was a pain that stretched *waaaay* back. That memory nearly threw her out of bed. The pillows and cushions scattered. The alarm clock at her elbow fell over and buzzed in unscheduled rage. Hannah flicked on the lamp and her cell phone in two-fisted, ambidextrous panic. Had she ever, ever told Isabel this story? Across the room, the lights of northwest D.C. shone at her window in pre-midnight flicker and wave: not too late to call her lover. The illumination of the Washington National Cathedral did not dim until midnight, Eastern Standard Time. As she focused her eyes to tap Isabel's private number onto fogged glass, the phone rang. Hannah squeaked.

"It's me, love. It's Isabel. What's keeping you awake?"

Of course, even all those miles away, Isabel knew she was troubled and needed to talk. "It's something surfacing from the past. Like a nasty humpback whale."

"Your own history? So, this is not a playful phone call." Isabel's voice, gentle. "No erotica by phone tonight."

"No," Hannah agreed regretfully. "Another time. Listen, you know how I'm involved in this—this project, with lesbian books? Looking at how many were banned, or restricted, so gay kids couldn't get them? I mean, we all talked about that at Halloween, and that was great. But I think I left out some pretty important questions, and now I'm stuck here and can't get to the bar to ask our friends again."

"What did you forget to ask? Don't be so hard on yourself."

"I, I asked everyone about their first encounter with a gay book, and their first encounter with asking a

126

librarian for one—how anyone got the life-altering book they really wanted or needed. But I forgot to ask what anyone's first memory was of book banning—if they remembered those certain parents, those certain *moms* who kept the books out of the schools."

Isabel kept quiet for a moment. Then, "Yes, the book-banning women. Well, you will find, very fresh in the minds of some still living, stories of mothers and daughters in the Third Reich burning books together. There are photos of that, too, easily researched, especially where you are, in those museums. But I think you have your own book-banning memory to share. That's it, isn't it?"

"Did I ever tell you about Jordan Matthews's mom?"

And when she opened her lips, her mind, to recall that memory, Sappho's mysterious projector turned on. Winged Sappho landed on the scattered pillows of Hannah's sofa bed and on the one blank wall opposite, where Hannah for some reason had yet to hang a poster, the past's slide show began. The Overhead Herself spread light around Hannah, who huddled up in bed, as Sappho ran the slide show of her past, screenshots of a young Hannah in 1975.

1975. At fourteen, a young and confused Hannah would have marched for gay and lesbian rights but punched out anyone who dared call her a dyke. Too soon to claim that name, too soon to act on love, but too soon to *feel* the love that dared not speak its name? No, she did that every day, her best friend's fate linked to hers, their private understanding an enigma to the school. They carved a wide swath in the halls, ebullient, untouchable. Not touching, leaving one another notes. In code. *Jill.*

A few adults did understand: three hip counselors who staffed a drop-in center at the school. There, amid the at-risk kids and other gay-maybes, Hannah had found her first books about the range of human sexuality. And there, on the "graffti wall" sheet of paper, she had tentatively scrawled with ink markers her best friend's name. In code. But the youth counselor had told her, "Hannah, your touch touches me."

In that drop-in center a unique cross-section of students laughed and cried and argued: Hannah and Jill, the tough girls and the disaffected guys, the kids with drug problems and hard parents. "Here come Hannah and Jill," shouted some when they arrived, acknowledging their partnership and even welcoming their wisdom.

Sometimes they did games and exercises from the book called *Values Clarification,* the book that was really "in" that year. Martin or Luke or Debra picked sample games or questions for discussion; these were called "energizers." Where would you go if you could go anywhere? Which person do you most like or admire? What is something you're proud of? What's hardest for you? Who do you really trust? Every answer Hannah provided somehow included Jill's name. Everything, for her, led back to loving Jill.

Sometimes the discussions were serious rap sessions about school: If you see a classmate cheating, should you tell, or is that ratting? How do you handle peer pressure to do drugs? Do students have the right to protest unannounced inspection of their lockers? Should students be suspended for holding sit-ins in the cafeteria?

Occasionally, there were worksheets that went with these discussions. Unfortunately, after one particularly cool discussion about sex, moral choices, and adult hypocrisy, a kid took his worksheet home in his book-bag, a parent saw the worksheet, and all hell broke loose.

By sheer accident, Hannah and Jill had been attending PTA meetings that winter quarter because Hannah's mother was on a policy committee, and she'd invited their input. That next PTA executive board meeting unfolded like a plain old bread sandwich at first, giving Hannah and Jill ample time to practice sitting up straight like obedient, A-plus students. Hannah's mother sat a few feet away from them, doodling on a pad. Teachers droned about the school semester and the activities budget. Parents coughed and touched their hairdos, waiting for the moment when they could introduce new issues. Unlike the adults, who counted as actual people, Hannah and Jill weren't offered the courtesy of name tags, so Hannah made a large sign with both their names, *Hannah + Jill*, and propped it up on the table. This certainly made them look like a married couple, but by the time Hannah realized that, it seemed too late to crumple up the banner and start over with separate signs.

Hannah whispered to Jill, "Yawn! Executive *b-o-r-e-d* meeting!" When would the adults shut up so they could speak? They had specifically attended this meeting in order to praise the work of the student drop-in center. Those youth counselors were absent tonight, waiting to give a prepared presentation at next week's "open" PTA meeting, but Hannah hoped to show the executive board some preliminary student support from two "responsible"-type students who actively used the center.

Parents and teachers began arguing about the gifted-and-talented program, which had never been launched. Hannah and Jill, who knew they were

129

among those classified as "gifted" students, watched in disgust as adults once again killed off the funding for their enrichment.

Suddenly, a well-dressed mother stood up and began to speak.

"I have been a teacher for twenty years myself," she began. "My name is Mrs. Matthews. Perhaps the other parents here aren't aware of how our school system is changing, but I am here tonight to tell you that certain people are using our students as unwitting tools to radicalize our society. There is evil at work in the so-called Student Drop-In Center. Certain books available to vulnerable young people need to be removed. Immediately."

Hannah and Jill looked at each other in shock, completely unprepared for this.

"This secular humanist way of teaching sets no goals, has no rights or wrongs, no absolute values," Mrs. Matthews continued. "Our children are being taught only to worry about their own friends, their own feelings. Mrs. Nash and I are part of a group called Parents Concerned, which opposes these anti-Christian philosophies, viewpoints, and activities ongoing in the center. We intend to see the center shut down."

There was absolute silence for some minutes.

Then a father raised his hand. "What are your specific objections? My kid hangs out at the center all the time; I had no idea anything dangerous went on there. It's officially a part of the school, isn't it?"

"Yes, indeed," Mrs. Nash chimed in; she had popped up beside Mrs. Matthews and now wore the same pinched expression on her face. "And did you know it was school policy to expose your child to the alarmingly gross secular humanist book *Values Clarification*? No? A story inviting students to discuss sex choices? If you were truly permitted to be a concerned parent in this anti-Christian school system, the PTA board would mandate that only children with parental permission slips could enter Student Resources for these secular humanistic exercises."

Hannah heard her science teacher hiss to a colleague, "Oh, my god. That's Mrs. Nash. She tried to have me fired two years ago when I assigned my eighth-graders a term paper on evolution." Hannah wondered if this was the real reason why Mr. Zeph now used those cautious, uninteresting mimeographed handouts for his classwork.

"The staff of Student Resources have come into Eastern Junior High, unasked, to seize control of our students' minds," Mrs. Matthews was saying. "Humanism has been declared a religion by the courts, and it is being used on our children. We know that those staff members plan to be at next week's PTA meeting to present their agenda, and we plan to be there—all of us in Parents Concerned. That student center is unnecessary and dangerous. And if you are responsible parents, you'll band together and help us."

She drew herself up and exploded, "Vain-brain perverts fill our children with conceit, trying to bring about a new social order and *world plan* of love, love, love! Love for betrayers of our values! Their humanistic principles include autonomy and full sexual freedom for everyone!"

The room erupted as parents, teachers, and officials all began to argue at once. Mrs. Matthews and Mrs. Nash shook their fingers; the PTA president called for order. None of the student drop-in center staff were present to defend the center. No one in the room but Hannah and Jill had ever used the space or its small library. No one was asking for their opinion now. These were the adults empowered to make decisions about their lives?

As brainy girls, they often experienced this strange and embarrassing epiphany, of realizing that they were already smarter than any number of grown-ups they knew. Their minds were clicking along analytically, pinpointing the holes in Mrs. Matthews' arguments. Every ninth-grader at Eastern Junior High had just completed the Speech and Debate unit in English class that month, and it was impossible not to apply that rhetoric to the highly political conflict unfurling in the room. *Resolved: banning books is a threat to our democracy* . . .

They began writing notes back and forth, under the table, in Hannah's journal, while the adults called one another names. *We are surrounded. And their arguments are not credible.*

Suddenly, in front of everyone, Jill put her arm around Hannah, and kept it there for the rest of the meeting. It was a protective statement, not a romantic one, but Hannah's mind and heart went racing. Was this Jill's way of standing up to Mrs. Matthews, of valorizing love over close-mindedness? Was this Jill's way of being visible, of declaring that she had someone who cared about her? Jill never held her like this at school. Yet there they were, at the big, round table in the school library, surrounded by symbols of authority: Parents. Teachers. Encyclopedias. And in that space, claiming her own authority, just this once, Jill held Hannah, while the adults debated book banning.

Hannah had felt herself growing larger by the minute, like Alice in Wonderland. In calm tones, she began to speak, defending Student Resources and its staff, its small lending library. Her history teacher, a rather elegantly brilliant old woman, moved her

132

coiffed head slowly up and down as Hannah spoke. But Mrs. Matthews stared hatefully at Hannah. This was Jordan Matthews's mom; Jordan was a nondescript good student and basketball captain, friendly to everyone.

Then Hannah jumped up and ran out into the hallway, into what they all called *the bad girl bathroom*, now empty of students. As she hid her face in a stall and cried silently, the door to that bathroom opened and two sets of heels clicked in furiously. Hannah pressed herself, unseen, invisible, to the dank tile wall, and listened to the adult female intruders' muttered words.

"I think a seed was planted here tonight," said Mrs. Nash.

"But those two little girls stick together like flypaper," sneered Mrs. Matthews.

Like flypaper. Mrs. Matthews. Mother of Jordan Matthews. She changed everything.

"I grew up that night. That minute," Hannah told Isabel, now, so many decades later. "I went up to bed that night and I lay awake pie-eyed. *Little girl?* I was already five foot six and wore 30/32 Levis. I wore a size eight soccer cleat and could kick the damn ball, too. I'd had my period for two and a half years. I could give birth, be a mother myself. *Like flypaper.* Flypaper was something I associated with vermin, with ugliness; it symbolized unwelcome, invasive pests. It was what you used up and threw away when you wanted to purify, to exterminate the insects in your home. This was how they saw Jill and I, and our loving friendship: we were damaging little flies, a secular humanistic plague unleashed by Student Resources, a sticky problem for good Christians.

133

Anyway, it didn't stop there. That committee sent out a newsletter to every parent in the school, and after more meetings our school did ban some books."

Isabel's quiet breathing on the other end of the phone. Then: "You see how *this* made you into the book protector you are, the out and proud defender of lesbian books for youth."

"I didn't know what to do with my rage," Hannah remembered now. "You forget how disempowered you are, at fourteen. No income, no car, no Internet then, so no blog, no Facebook, no social media. No private cell phone, no way to connect broadly with other 'questioning' youth. I wrote in my journal and I played Grace Slick over and over on my stereo, that song where she snarls, 'Consider how small you are. Compared to your scream, the human dream doesn't mean shit to a tree.' That scream, that swear word—all I had."

"No other women's music yet, either," Isabel mused.

Hannah brightened. "But there *was*. That was when I found it on the radio. That very night! It was The Deadly Nightshade, 'High Flying Woman.' I heard three women's voices, deep and confident—'I'm Helen,' 'I'm Ann.' 'I'm Pam.' They sang,

Did you ever think that you lived in a cage?
Did you ever think that you lived in a cage?
Well, they're calling you a "chick,"
And the name just seems to stick,
And you still don't think you're living in a cage?

Have you heard, have you heard,
There's a migration happening:
Going where the thinking is free.
Only you can decide,

Take yourself for a glide;
You're a free-flying woman
A high-flying woman.

"You became a high-flying woman that night. Yes. But then what happened? Is there more?" Isabel probed. And Sappho cupped Hannah's head.

"What else about Jordan Matthews?" Isabel asked. "Mrs. Matthews' daughter. Your classmate. Probably not easy for her, to be the child of book-banning campaigners."

"I don't know. She had no part in their activism. Jordan was quiet at school, mostly involved with team sports—actually, captain of everything. She always had a splinted sports injury, rushing from one practice to another, wore athletic clothes every day, at a time and place where most girls were either sexy, hippie, or square in style. She walked like a jock. God, I never thought about it before, but Jordan, well, wasn't exactly girlish. You never saw her in a dress, though her parents were these well-known conservative fundamentalists."

Such familiar details, insignificant until now, blazed along Hannah's neurons in an instant. And Hannah *recognized* her. Recognized a sister. Jordan was going to grow up and be *gay*.

That was Jordan in my memory of going to the library and searching for gay books. That was Jordan in the other aisle, apart from me and also hiding there. That was Jordan I saw when I let myself go back and remember— and what I saw was Jordan lifting books. Stealing what she needed to find out about herself.

"What if your parents had been the ones to suppress gay-sympathetic books in school? Wouldn't your adolescent rebellion take the form of reading those books under the covers by flashlight? Or maybe there would be no way, in those days before ordering online, to get the books you needed. If you grew up gay in that household, wouldn't you be likely to amass the world's best collection of lesbian books as an adult? And in your better days as an aging adult, might you not take steps to pass those books back into another school library?" As Isabel spoke, Sappho turned off the projector. The light of the Overhead Herself withdrew, leaving shimmering scales as slides of Hannah's past faded. It was past midnight; in Washington, D.C., the lights of the National Cathedral also blinked out, leaving an absence that almost pulsed. Hannah sat in total darkness, feeling the trajectory of life that had taken her to Isabel, from campaigning for books in ninth grade to saving books at the Library of Congress.

"You don't need me to facilitate time travel," Isabel spoke softly. "You carry your own timeline in your heart. And you know what to do. You can make that phone call to the donor, now. But make it from the bad girl bathroom, if you follow what I mean. Good night, my dear one."

And as Isabel's voice faded out on the cell phone, every hair stood up on Hannah's flesh. She knew who the Library's mystery book donor was. The donor was Jordan Matthews.

Chapter Seven

The Donor's Legacy

That spring was filled with work, projects and exhibits that demanded attention, leaving no time or privacy for sleuthing around the donation of books. Hannah was now desperate on two fronts. Her job would end in May, and she had one crate of books under the bed of her rented apartment, books stolen from a Library of Congress van and intended for readers *out there somewhere*. She also had to get back to the loading dock area and rescue the other box of books, hidden under the old glue machine—the box of paperbacks from the donor that *someone* on staff had separated out to be shredded.

When Hannah finally had a free moment to retrieve the original donation paperwork, she discovered that the entire file had been moved to a different department. With the help of a box of Godiva chocolates from the Union Station galleria, she bribed two different library employees in order to get one more glance at the donation cover sheet.

No, there was no contact phone number or e-mail. Yes, the donor's initials were J.M. no, the donor was not deceased. This was a living legacy.

Jordan was still alive. And, quite possibly, not dying or even ill, just willing to place a great collection where it might reach the maximum number of patrons . . . or so Jordan had thought. How could Hannah tell her that there was, in fact, no solid plan to make those books available to needy readers? How to find the generous Jordan in the first place? What was Hannah supposed to *do?*

By Thursday, Hannah had a range of archival tasks that permitted one long break in the afternoon. She worked steadily with head bowed, shrinking into herself as if to will inconspicuousness. She had dressed deliberately, that day, in a mild beige sweater with no flashy scarf, no jingling jewelry. Willing herself into relative invisibility, she began her break time by walking on tiptoe through the Great North Hall where the artistic portrait of Sappho appeared on the ceiling, one lone woman among the many male authors depicted. *Sappho. Point the way. Project the Overhead's way for me.*

And the way became clearer. She saw, thanks to Sappho, a strange little scene that had taken place months before: a stoic warehouse worker named Gordon falling more and more under the influence of a local megachurch pastor whose homophobic sermons were legendary in northern Virginia.

She saw Gordon, assigned the task of readying two crates of rare lesbian books for off-site storage, balking at the idea of helping circulate such filth. Gordon, on his own coffee break time, tossing what he found to be the "worst" of such sinful sex material into one of the send-to-the-shredder boxes. Gordon, caught in the act, confronted by Al, the kindly driver of the van Hannah had been in. She saw Al, a defender of books, a First Amendment T-shirt tucked tight over his belly, gently moving the terrified paperbacks to a safe spot and then marching Gordon down to Human Resources and having him fired, with the recycling pickup representative arriving just at that minute and starting to load the condemned books onto a flatbed meant for the shredder. Jay, a concerned coworker of Al's, was yelling, "No! Not that one," and grabbing the box off the flatbed, locking it up somewhere.

Oh, no! Moved? Where? Locked? How? Hannah sped up her steps. She made a mental note to send both Al and Jay thank-you letters and candy at some future moment, much buoyed by this peek into the heroism of male colleagues protecting lesbian literature. *Where would a guy hide lesbian paperbacks?*

She didn't dare ask them. Everything now depended on her anonymity, on not attracting attention. *Maybe not in the loading dock area itself. Maybe he tucked that box into his own office and has since forgotten all about it. Or what if he took it home? Like I did?*

But when Hannah peered through the open door into the loading dock area, she encountered a familiar scent. Coffee. Isabel's beans! The little table area where the workers took their coffee break was crowded with large, belt-wearing men just now, all hoisting coffee cups or stirring in cream and sugar. Piles of unwashed mugs and baskets of sugar substitute covered one end of the table, and an open box of doughnuts commanded attention at the table's opposite end.

As men swarmed around their snacks and then walked away, Hannah caught one clear glimpse of something pushed partway under the table. There, in the shadows, long neglected, was the controversial box of donated books that Jay had thought to hide. It had not been destroyed, or lost, or shredded after all!

But as Hannah began to rise from her crouched position, she abruptly recoiled. Only at ground level could one see what thoughtful Jay had done to keep the books from being seized by other fundamentalists. He had secured the crate of books to a post under the table with an old combination lock.

Hannah slumped to the floor, never minding that other librarians might pass by any minute and ask her what she was doing there. *Foiled.* This was an impossibility. What had she been thinking—that she would just waltz in one evening after hours and pry open a locked crate? How would she ever break that lock or, at best, plunder an opened crate to "rescue" the books? Exactly where would she be moving them to?

This notion—that there existed some mystical plain of needy young lesbian readers, into whose outstretched hands she might place appropriate banned literature—this notion existed only in her mind. There was no such assembled, physical audience in the present day, and gay teens of the past were unreachable. This was the wrong library for her sentimental, idealistic activism. And there on the cold floor of an otherwise very good library, Hannah wept for the loss of feminist bookstores, for the digitizing of literature that made once-priceless paperbacks mere pulp.

Sudden footsteps approaching from the next corridor reminded her that she wasn't truly alone and had better exit the shipping area. With a last peek at the locked crate, Hannah rose from the scholarly dust and headed to her sanctuary: the visitors' bathroom and pay phone. That space would tell her what to do.

She walked numbly to the front hall of the Jefferson Building and the familiar door to that well-tiled restroom. Her palm hit the surface. But what opened to her eyes when she entered was not the Library of Congress ladies' room, at all.

It was the bad-girl bathroom of her old junior high.

The pay phone was still there, in its half-enclosed wall booth, yet behind it Hannah saw the graffiti-scrawled stalls and ash-sopped paper towels of her ninth-grade school building. Defiant cigarette butts and marijuana roaches peeped from cracks in the floor tile, and smoke lingered in the air, but there was something else. A peculiar, *adult* smell of what young Hannah had always thought of as "old lady" perfume.

Her first panicked reaction was to think that one of her old teachers, too, had blundered into this most off-limits of student hideaways. But that never would have happened; teachers had their own bathroom in the faculty lounge. Hannah poked her head inside the nearest stall to see if any living human were inside.

As she did, fascinated to see that the same graffiti she remembered from 1975 was still on the back wall, she heard two toilets flush; two pairs of heels clicked toward the exit, and she heard the familiar, heart-stopping words: "Those two little girls stick together like flypaper."

Hannah burst out of the stall. Was she really back in 1975, humiliated in this same bathroom after that rancorous PTA meeting? She looked down at her body, afraid it might be her younger teenage self, clad in the faded Levis she had worn that night so long ago. But there, so reassuring now, were her plain work pants of adulthood, and her Library of Congress ID was still clipped to the belt. She ran her tongue over her teeth; no retainer, thank god, another good sign. She rolled up her left shirt sleeve; yes, the tattoo from her fortieth birthday was still there. She was grown Hannah, modern Hannah, transported to this rest-room nightmare of her past.

And then the pay phone rang. The haunted pay phone, also nailed against this daydream. She grabbed for it, dry-mouthed, her unbuttoned shirt sleeve flapping. "Hello."

"This is Jordan," said the donor. "You need to save those books."

"It's Jordan," the voice told her again, and now they were back in the regular women's room of the Library of Congress, with one or two visitors innocently coming and going, straightening hairclips or stepping into stalls as Hannah bent into the phone's receiver. "I remember you."

"I remember you, too," Hannah managed to say.

"You can figure out the combination on that crate— it's not hard. And there's a way to shelve those books where anyone can get them. Will you do that?"

"Jordan, where are you?" Hannah asked her. "Are you—are you well? Are you in Washington? Could we meet, can you tell me more about what happened in your life? After—after you came out?"

"Oh, I'm very much alive, but not in Washington. Just off the grid, you know, living in a cabin that I built. I'm happy," Jordan affirmed, with a voice radiating grit and triumph, untroubled by the past.

"I found the love I wanted, and can return the books I had to have before. Did you ever take a book out of the library and keep it, long overdue? Then lie and tell the librarian you lost it, just so you could have it for yourself? I did that many times. I paid the fines at twenty-five libraries, every time we moved, and then in college. It wasn't much money; I had two jobs, and didn't mind the payments. But later I thought, my god. Who else needed all the books I hoarded? So. This donation is action *overdue*. You get my meaning? I'm overdue with everyone. I'm overdue with God."

"The Overhead," Hannah heard herself say. "She placed me here."

"And She'll set up the shelf you need for putting back

my books. You are going to do a Grand Reshelving, friend. Every book back in its place, available for other kids in that kind of private, desperate, coming-out search.

"On the right night, you need to be at work ready to do that reshelving. Then I'll really be at peace, and I can't tell you how I know this, but I can pretty much guarantee the books will be checked out immediately, each to the best owner, and the whole shelf will vanish again without a trace. You won't be in trouble." She actually laughed. "There won't be a *paper* trail."

"But how, Jordan? When?" Hannah looked over her shoulder at her favorite security guard, who had just stepped into the bathroom to splash water on her face. "How is this going to work? Can't you explain?"

"I always thought you were kinda nice," Jordan told her, playful now, and fading out in voice. "I wasn't wrong. I liked you. My parents had their demons. Most of mine are gone. Just save the books and shelve them!" And the line went dead.

That night, Hannah called Isabel at Sappho's Bar and Grill, knowing it would be packed there on a Friday night with the regular crowd—the same women she had talked to on Halloween weekend. Isabel answered immediately, "Sappho's. Is this my sweetheart calling?"

"Yes. Hi, honey. Um, can you do me a favor? If you're not busy."

The ringing of a cash register, shouts of laughter, the beat of "We Are Family." She could so easily picture it all. "I'm busy, but I'm glad to do you a favor," Isabel answered, calling out bar orders. "Genny Cream Light. Two Labatt Blues. Seven and Seven. Black Russian. Moira, can you take over? Hannah, what's your question?"

Hannah had to smile at Isabel's swift understanding that she had one final query for the bar. "Please ask anyone within earshot if they ever *stole* a book, a library book, or kept it long past overdue, because they *had to have a lesbian book* in their possession."

It took a few minutes for this message to circulate around the bar, and Hannah fixed herself a drink of her own in the tiny kitchen of her D.C. rental while her ear soaked up the sounds of happy hour at Sappho's. Then:

"Sure, I did it," rasped the bold voice of Letty. "I kept back that one, I think it was Gertrude Stein. No one else had ever checked it out in all the years of our town library—I don't know how they ever ordered it in the first place. But since mine was the only scrawl on the checkout card in the back of the book I didn't dare return it, 'cause then everyone would know I was the town dyke. I kept it under my bed in a shoebox with my cigs and a movie-star picture of Sophia Loren."

"Give me that phone." This was Trale. "We kept some of what wasn't ours but it *was* ours; we needed it like oxygen. Can I tell you a line from Mary Daly? 'We righteously plunder what has been stolen from women.' I heard her say that at a rally and she meant that we had to steal back our history, or herstory. I stole two books, the one on women in carpentry—it was called *Against the Grain*—and the one by Judy Grahn, *The Work of a Common Woman*. I put them back, though, when I turned sixty and downsized all my stuff."

Then, Dog. "I was busted for shoplifting, but a library book? Huh. You know, I think I did keep an overdue one—*Oranges Are Not the Only Fruit*. I remember because my dad whaled me for the fine that showed up on his account. I was using his card

144

for my homework. I lied and said it was all a mistake. I gave him the cost of the book for the library, from my babysitting money . . ."

She heard shrieks of derision. "You were a baby-sitter?" "Can you imagine Dog as your babysitter? I would have loved that!" "I wouldn't leave *my* kid with Dog!"

But she had her answer, or answers. Almost every woman had secretly ripped off a lending library in sheer desperate need to have a baby-dyke book. There had been in these women's lives local feminist book-stores, even mail-order catalogues, in those years before the Internet. But few had had cars or, more likely the nerve, at fifteen and sixteen and seventeen, to get to a lesbian bookshop if they were fortunate enough to live near one. *Borrowing* became *owning*. "We were all criminals anyway," Yvette told Hannah, now. "I mean, what was one more entry on the outlaw resume?"

"I was a *felon* in Virginia," Carol grabbed the phone. "Standing to lose custody, job, housing, due to those damn sodomy laws. Add unpaid library fines, and you see why I left the state altogether."

"Okay. I just wondered. But can any of you tell me," Hannah wound up her long-distance interrogation, "*where* all those overdue books are now?"

"Garage sales?" "The Lesbian Herstory Archives?" "Attic of my parents' summer house?" Many were the guesses shouted toward the phone; yet no one was quite sure.

"But you felt you had to have those books, to survive?" Isabel finished for Hannah. And hundreds of miles away, through the receiver of her phone, Hannah heard the great response in unison, "*Yes.*"

☙ ☙ ☙

Two hours later, drunk on a second martini assembled from one of Isabel's special mixes stocked in her dollhouse-sized refrigerator, Hannah called the Snerd. "How do you break a combination lock?"

Silence. Then, "Last time it was cloning the dead from drool. Now it's safecracking. Can't you get a job?"

"I had one," Hannah snarled. "Teaching women's history. Remember? *That* job disappeared. I'm in exile, doing what I can. Listen, I can't explain what this is all about; just know I'm saving books right now. Books that might have a particular meaning for young women on the verge of coming out."

"Books you wish that *you* had read in college? What's driving you to do this?" It was unusual for the Snerd to ask Hannah's opinion, so she considered her response carefully for a quiet moment. The line between them, Washington to Oakland, crackled and hummed.

"Well, what are you doing in that lab?" Hannah finally asked, knowing Jade couldn't reveal her protocol.

"I can't spill the protocol, dope, but you know. Trying to find a cure for a certain kind of human suffering."

"Exactly," Hannah shouted. "I can't spill my details either. I'm also trying to find a cure for human suffering. We both went into work that has a purpose. Mine doesn't have a lab."

And with that, the Overhead Projector turned on. The wall opposite Hannah's sofabed shimmered with an unexpected slide show: Hannah and Jade "The Snerd" in college, friends, not lovers. But that year Hannah had been in love with Jade Wing. And by some miracle of timing they had studied the work of Wu Zao, the great lesbian poet of China, in the one class they shared: a multicultural women's studies course which for Jade was a nice break from premed labs. For Hannah, it was an awakening to women's history.

And on the day their professor, a salty older butch named Helene Barrad, read aloud Wu Zao's nineteenth-century love poem, "For the Courtesan Ch'ing Lin," Hannah had also awakened to the possibility of desire. Now Sappho's overhead projector showed Hannah and the Snerd open-mouthed in their seats, legs jiggling nervously from their worn Adidas to their parted knees, as Dr. Barrad intoned these lines:

> One smile from you when we meet,
> And I become speechless and forget every word . . .
> You glow like a perfumed lamp
> In the gathering shadows . . .
> I want to possess you completely—
> Your jade body
> And your promised heart.

Hannah had leaned across the aisle to whisper, "Your *jade* body," and the Snerd poked her with a mechanical pencil, hissing, "Shut up." Hannah scribbled on a corner of torn notebook paper, *Do you believe in reincarnation? You could be Wu Zao,* and Jade wrote back, *I am a Presbyterian. And you are no courtesan Ch'ing Lin. Plus, Hannah, for the last time: I. Am. STRAIGHT!*

On the back of the Snerd's note there were three figures: notes from chem class. Even that day, as Hannah had dreamed of desire and seduction, Jade had been elsewhere, scribbling formulae on her notepad, memorizing not poetry but the periodic table of the elements. It was that familiarity with numbers and symbols that Hannah needed now. Those numbers, those three numbers. She could almost see those numbers. But just then the slide show ended.

Their phone conversation resumed in the here and now.

"See, there's a padlock around these books. A combination lock. Wouldn't that be three numbers? 9, 10, 7? A three-part code? You're the formula expert. I'm stumped. I can't guess it."

"Yes, a three-part combination would release the tumblers, and no, I can't offer you any help beyond that, darling. I'm trying to get a *grant*. I can't be cracking safes in federal buildings. Look, call me in daylight sometime. Why are you always up at one in the morning?"

Hannah put the phone back on her nightstand. As she did, a tiny piece of paper blew off the tabletop and onto her blanket. It was the number of the bathroom pay phone, which she had copied down back in the fall and tried calling from her own apartment to see if it truly was in service.

It blazed at her like lightning now. That number held the code.

Then the phone rang again in Hannah's apartment: The Snerd, calling back. She lifted the phone to her ear.

"Forgot to tell you," whispered her old friend. "That strand of hair you sent? I had it tested. It must have come into the Library pressed between the pages of a really old book. That's the only explanation, because—"

And she told Hannah what she'd learned.

The next day, trembling, Hannah stayed after work, slipped into the loading dock, and hid under the old glue machine with a door-sized piece of cardboard over her body until the lights went out and the last worker had departed. She listened for any sound or sign of a remaining staff member: papers being shuffled, keys on a belt, a cleared throat. After thirty full minutes of silence, she crept out and found the coffee table (flecked with crumbs). Beneath it, shoved one foot back where Jay had forgotten all about it, was Jordan's crate.

The padlock was an ordinary one and secured the box to a heating pipe. She knelt before the crate. *Three numbers.* Her first instinct was to go to the obvious. 3-0-1. The section of the local library where, at fourteen, she'd first found books about lesbians, that day she'd spotted Jordan Matthews lurking, one shelf over, when both their home area codes were 301.

But the padlock wouldn't budge. 301 was wrong.

Her mind raced across history. Three numbers representing lesbians. Numbers that meant lesbian books? Which book titles included numbers? Her anxiety turned swiftly to affection as she made a mental list of titles in Jordan's collection: Rita Mae Brown, *Six of One.* Adrienne Rich, *Twenty-one Love Poems.* Red Arobateau, *Six Stories.* But no. 6-21-6 failed.

Then she turned to the phone booth's number—much more than three single numbers, but in three clear parts: 202-554-4876. This had to contain the solution, and she stared at it blurrily until one possibility emerged. The numbers in each section added up to something else, creating a second list of three. Two plus 0 plus 2. 5 plus 5 plus 4. 4 plus 8 plus 7 plus 6. She added and scribbled, then sucked in her breath, hopeful.

Now she had: 4, 14, 25.

That was it.

She was sure, now, her fingers spinning confidently. But the lock stayed closed. *Not fair!* her heart cried out. *I know it's the phone number! Three parts! I figured it out! Why won't it work? I'm losing time here! Overhead— Sappho—Isabel—help me!*

She shut her eyes. Then Hannah understood. She had to add those numbers one more time. Four, 14, 25 should be 4, then 1 plus 4, then 2 plus 5—making the absolute final reduction 4, 5, 7. Was that it?

It was. The lock sprang open in her hand, and with it a sigh of impossible relief from the fluttering books inside.

Now Hannah had to think and move fast. These books had to be scooped out and hidden somewhere else that night, and the padlock closed again. There were at least fifty paperback books, fortunately not as heavy as their hardcover sisters, those books meant for off-site storage that Hannah had instead lugged home. She had two shopping bags from Trader Joe's stuffed under her jacket, as well as her backpack, and quickly spread them out and began apportioning books in each. Even in the urgency of this mission, she couldn't help feeling awed affection for each classic: the Mexican edition of Rita Mae Brown's *Rubyfruit Jungle,* its Spanish title *Frutos de Rubi;* Katherine Forrest's *Curious Wine.*

Then, with backpack full and a bag slung over each shoulder, Hannah moved quietly to the door, which was of course locked now but, thankfully, opened again from the inside. It wasn't late. There were still many Library staff about, plus early evening security guards coming on shift. Hannah made sure her ID badge was visible as she stepped into the corridor. Now, where to stash the gold mine?

The answer was absurdly obvious: her own office desk. Aurora left early every day, so that was no concern, but what about the other archivists? Hannah decided to take the stairs, though her hip sockets ached already from the weight of books distributed around her middle-aging body. When had she last worked out in a gym? *Up. Up.* She'd better start lifting weights again if she was going to reshelve all these books at some mystical point in the future. Her knees creaked. But as she rounded the final corner to reach her own floor, she distinctly felt one of the books in her knapsack shift forward and pat her on the back.

No one around.

Go.

Feeling like she was in a complex Hollywood movie (*Harry Potter? Night at the Museum? The Pink Panther?*), Hannah sidestepped down the hall to her office area, key between her fingers. The lights were off—an excellent sign. She was alone! Quickly, she unlocked the door and then locked it again behind her, keeping the light switch off and taking silent but giant steps toward her work cubicle.

Problem: in this era of digital storage, Hannah's desk had only two drawers. Not nearly enough room for fifty books.

There was, however, a file cabinet that no one ever used in the supply closet. Hannah noticed it each time she went in there for a fresh pen or photocopier paper. But what if her coworkers thought to peek into that file cabinet one day? She'd have to risk it, with some sort of disguise. Hannah moved the books to the closet, realizing the irony of bold lesbian lives temporarily being forced "back in the closet" in order to survive. How often had that happened to books, or authors, or actual women? *This will be the last time, I promise you,* she thought. She hoped.

It was easy enough to line the empty file cabinet with books. Next, she took sheets of light blue paper, which were hardly ever used in the photocopier, and covered the books, several inches high. On top of that she stacked accounting forms, old posters from the Christmas exhibit and, finally, open cardboard boxes full of magic markers, erasers and rubber bands.

There! No one would guess, if they ever went into the file cabinet drawers at all, that Jordan Matthews's life as a desperate young reader and book thief was secretly waiting there, waiting for release and redistribution.

Hannah refolded the empty shopping bags and left them in her desk, shouldered her regular work briefcase and walked out of her office, locking the door securely behind her. She waved calmly at coworkers emerging after late workdays from their own offices: "Have a good night." *But what might they have been up to, staying late after work? Who really knew?*

On the ground floor, just before the exit where she would surrender her (empty) workbag to be searched, the haunted bathroom beckoned. Hannah hesitated. She'd had enough. But she could hear the pay phone ringing faintly. Grinding her teeth, she stepped inside and seeing only normal and pristine emptiness, reached for the phone.

They were all cheering her, whistling and hooting, a chorus of butch voices from the literary past. It was another party of the banned authors, the ones who had written the books Hannah had saved.

"Yes, you saved us," shouted one. "Good job!" "But it's so cramped in this file drawer!" teased another. Hannah heard corks popping, backs being slapped, the smack of blown kisses. *"Mmwah!"*

The phone abruptly went dead. Now the ringing began directly in Hannah's ears. She dropped the receiver and backed away, holding her head. The light in the bathroom changed to amber, to gold; and then Sappho was at the sink, unfolding her wings.

"Go home and sleep your best," said Sappho. "Prepare yourself for the Grand Reshelving. It will take place on March 8, International Women's Day." She drew into herself and, just before she disappeared, one long wing brushed against the sink. In that act of contact between the fixed and the possible, Hannah understood who, or what, had left behind one dark hair in that sink. It came from Sappho's wing; and only another wing, Jade Wing, the Snerd, would ever know the truth.

Chapter Eight

The Grand Reshelving

March 8, International Women's Day.

It was two weeks before the cherry blossoms would burst into soft beauty, ringing the monuments and luring so many tourists the Tidal Basin could not contain their numbers. Three weeks before Passover and the storyline of Hannah's foremothers. The eighth of March was not a women's day for Americans alone, but a date for the women of the world. Still not a "real" holiday, though, on the U.S. federal calendar, so Hannah had to go to work, pretending to be normal, expecting to stay late. The Grand Reshelving had to be done at an hour she couldn't imagine, since it did not exist in fixed time. Through the long day of assigned errands, she avoided the ground-floor bathroom.

Then, after work, having hidden in the supply closet barely breathing until receding shadows told her it was dark in Washington, Hannah carefully retrieved the books that she had hidden in that closet and in her desk, adding them to the books hidden below her bed since fall, which she had stuffed into her backpack and brought back in over a series of days.

She awaited the call, that she knew would come on the pay phone, and readied the odd tools at her disposal: extra keys and ID cards, soft shoes that wouldn't squeak on stairs or in remote rooms, a ridiculous but somehow sexy face mask she'd bought at the Spy Museum, a penlight, two book-bags and her camping backpack frame, now each bulging with the paperbacks designated for shredding and recycling. That Jordan's donation would get to the right girls, once positioned on some magic shelf, she was certain. The banned authors had assured her this was so.

When the halls sounded absolutely silent, Hannah began her fateful walk down several flights of stairs, and approached the women's bathroom with her packs.

No one was there, of course, and she settled into the stall closest to the pay phone, with one glance at her watch. Five hours left in March 8, Eastern Standard Time. Resting, then, on the cold tile floor of the bathroom, alert for any sound or movement—mice or security, phone-ring or federal building alarm—Hannah had all the time in the world to consider how many women had spent worried hours camped on bathroom floors. In such cramped, concerned vigilance, the homeless and addicted, the refugee and runaway had spent their harrowing nights of solitude and fear; in bathrooms like this one, desperate women had given birth, or miscarried alone, or overdosed. Women's history offered a sobering review of how every society treated its least valued: *women and children first!—unless you're poor, or brown, or undocumented, or hooked on drugs, or underage, or queer . . .*

Her mind wandered to more pleasant associations of women spending time in bathrooms. During the

1980s, every Monday night she and the women at Sappho's Bar had gathered to eat popcorn and watch *Cagney & Lacey*, the great female cop show which inevitably featured a moment of bathroom office work. "Conference, Christine!" Tyne Daly (as Lacey) would summon Sharon Gless (as Cagney), and the two would slam into the station ladies' room—where they had plenty of privacy, as the only two women, seemingly, employed as New York's Finest. The bathroom break allowed moral confrontations and abiding love pledged between two women on a job. In those episodes, American viewers glimpsed answers to questions percolating in a so-called postfeminist society: What are women *doing* in those long bathroom breaks? Applying makeup? Plotting castration? Nope: just figuring out how to deal with workplace sexism while seeming apolitical; how to balance doing the job twice as well to prove their femaleness is not a burden, with transcending harassment, low pay, danger, insult.

How they had cheered those bathroom scenes at Sappho's!

And—but the phone was ringing.

She leaped up, stumbling on one numb leg, banging into every sink in the lurch towards instruction. The phone felt warm, and emanated a smoky scent, as if it had been roasted over a campfire. She swallowed. "Hello."

"May 6, 1933!" crackled a horrible voice, and in the receiver, rushing toward her ear, the roar of a Nazi rally, the flames of burning books. Anguished voices crying for lost literature, yet unaware that what was still to come was burning flesh. This was the night of Magnus Hirschfeld's archive being burned, the great assembled library of gay and lesbian studies that existed at the time of Hitler's rise. For decades, the Institute for Sex Research in Berlin had been a focus for sex research by progressive scholars and sex activists. Perhaps 20,000 visitors a year came through the research library for its sources on the social acceptance of gay people and greater equality for women. Then, suddenly, in February of 1933 the Nazi Party banned publications on sex and gay advocacy groups. That May, German students announced their attack on the Institute. Thousands of Nazi youth jeered and cheered as "decadent" literature was pulled from the Institute's shelves, thrown into the streets, and set on fire. Gone in an instant were the carefully assembled bits and shards of what was known about gay lives—20,000 books and journals and photographs of LGBT lives. No scholar would have access to that knowledge again, or touch those pages; on that night in the Tiergarten of Berlin 40,000 mind-maddened onlookers championed the burning of "Jewish" literature. That moment presaged the burning, too, of gay and lesbian bodies, soon marched to concentration camps. No Overhead could change what Germany had done, with willing help from other fascist powers. In the great mourning of those lost lives was there even a moral space to crawl into, just to mourn the loss of those gay books?

These were the times when any hope of getting lesbian books to lesbian girls went up in smoke and into shit and worse. The phone burned on her ear.

Then a hand fell on her shoulder. A hard yet not unfriendly hand. And because it was a real hand of the here and now, attached to a real person in Washington who had joined her in the bathroom, it was far, far scarier than the wretched history of book destruction streaming from the phone.

The hand pulled Hannah around, and the phone fell from her grip. In front of her stood the security guard.

It was in fact her favorite guard, the one who was often in and out on a short break whenever Hannah was on the pay phone, and who had asked so long ago, "Does that old thing even work?" Her strong, dark face now expressionless, she aimed a flashlight directly into Hannah's eyes.

Caught at last. Hannah slumped against the pay phone, the receiver left dangling. Now the books would never be reshelved. Her entire mission was over—unfulfilled. She had failed the Overhead. She'd never work in this town again. Never in academia, never in any archive. Her mind raced for excuses—anything to avoid being arrested, having to call Isabel from jail.

"So—it's you," said the security guard, and a surprising corona of light appeared behind her head as her flashlight snapped off. "Finally! Well, we'd best get started, don't you think?" She leaned over and grabbed one of Hannah's bookbags.

"What—who are you?" Hannah gasped, and the guard, whose name tag had gone blank, expanded upward. She floated upward, in fact, one gracious extra length of height, so that she towered over Hannah, her sensible shoes no longer touching the floor. Floating ahead of Hannah, out of the bathroom, she tossed back over her broad shoulder, "Well, get a *clue*, girl! I'm your Crossing Guard. I work here for the Overhead. Like you."

᳕ ᳕ ᳕

Whatever her power, the Crossing Guard lived up to her title, as they exited the bathroom absolutely unnoticed by two other night watchmen despite (in Hannah's case) noisily ascending the stairs up to the Great North Hall. Once there, pausing at the display cases, the Crossing Guard snapped her fingers and suddenly they were on a different floor—a floor between floors, a floor that supposedly did not exist. It was part of no Library map Hannah had seen, and was perfectly clean and empty—but for the enormous hanging shelf that spun languidly in the midpoint of the space. They had crossed safely into this place.

Hannah felt a tiny and delicate tick at her wrist; her watch had stopped.

This was a shelf made of all the woods of the world: redwood, cedar, oak, cypress, mangrove, filling the air with magnificent scent. And all the wood that had ever been sacrificed for paper to make books stretched and reassembled into shelves that towered upward into skylight—impossible, thought Hannah, for were there not fixed Library of Congress floors, set above them? But in front of her were six floors' worth of bookshelf, and neither sky nor ceiling at the top.

She tiptoed closer. The pegs holding the shelf together jutted out in odd, soft nails that seemed to have a pattern, and she recognized Morse code, the code she'd used to signal her first love to her best friend. When language failed and outright declaration seemed too dangerous or wrong, they had used code. Now the shelf pegs in front of her spelled out the names of titles, categories, themes. She had a guide for organizing.

This was a shelf that appeared only at a fixed time, the time arranged by *She,* and Hannah understood it was a shelf not necessarily in the Library, but a part of the grand archiving and cataloguing and sorting made possible by all who served Her as radical librarians protective of woman's word, in every era where it met with scorn or burning, censorship or erasure, deplatforming or destruction. Hannah bowed low, and as she did so felt one tiny urgent *tick* at her wrist. She didn't have all the time in the world.

Pulling out the rare books she'd saved, smuggled and stolen, and unpacking all of them from her different bags, Hannah swiftly organized two piles, alphabetizing them by author name until Jordan's donation legacy was ready to reshelve. *Find me. Love me,* the books whispered as they settled in, each shaking their pages ever so slightly like the ruffling, preening feathers of proud exotic birds, preparing for flight—for a journey into time.

As she set them tenderly in order on the shelves, Hannah once again saw how influential these books had been in her own life—her own awakening. Each title carried a comet-trail of memories: here were the books that had been in her own bedroom when she was eighteen and reading voraciously anything she could find with the *L* word in its name.

The paper brushed over her. Ink touched her lips. She was standing still but stroked by pages. She had loved every one of these books; now, willing them to be loved by other women, other girls, she was sending them away. One familiar title popped out from the shelf as soon as she had placed it, begging, "Feel me up once more. . ." How that book had once seduced her, mentally, culturally, a lamp of light in years of wondering *how*. She had been . . . was being . . . here? Now? Oh! very gently fucked again by a book.

An intercom she could not see began to blare a teasing announcement: "Paging Dr. Stern. Paging Dr. Stern." Yes, she was being paged, old pages on her skin, moving across her heart. They were all around her, touching, stroking. An orgy of gratitude, of intimacy, of bookworm love. *Here!* urged a small paperback she hadn't touched yet. *Me, me!* The book cuddled against her hand, a feeling no less perfect than a lover's Sunday morning backrub. A larger volume bustled over, thick leather binding strap unhinging in slow motion, as trousers might be unbuckled by a patient, lovestruck butch. The opening of a chapter in that tome flexed like a bicep, and Hannah heard herself whisper, admiringly, "Show-off. How tough you are." The book glowed, its spine straight with near-military bearing, its brass buckle shiny. "Oh, you were the book with a uniform fetish." Hannah saluted, falling easily into old yet familiar tropes of flirtation from her earliest days.

Oh, was this delicious feeling an infidelity to Isabel, or the last lust of remembered adolescent bibliophilia? *Bibliogyne, you are mine,* the book spoke upward from between her hot breasts.

And then it said:

You will find the letter between pages 13 and 14 of your favorite book.

She shoved the book away in sudden alarm. Letter? What book? What pages?

Her letter, her letter, sighed the pages, ruffling, turning. The wind they stirred was just enough to lift Hannah's damp bangs, which fell again against her forehead as the book in her hands closed firmly and was silent.

Hannah thought, *But that's not possible. Books open flat with even numbers on the left, odd numbers on the right. There's no way to tuck a letter between a page 13 and a page 14!*

Possible indeed where we bind our own stories, came the answer. And the book in her hands fell quiet.

What was her favorite book? How could she ever, ever decide? How could she find out what this letter meant for her was? Hannah sat down on the polished floor of a nonexistent room. *Tick,* went her Seiko wristwatch.

But pages 13/14 . . . of course that was the age when she first thought, *perhaps I might be gay?* That was the year she dared to write the question in her journal. What was the book that seemed to reassure, the character she turned to? But there had been almost nothing, at that time, about fourteen-year-olds. She had written her own story, chronicled her own journey, in a notebook, like *Harriet the Spy.* She—

Harriet.

Hannah launched upward from the floor, knees cracking, and grabbed for the last of Jordan's books. There in the *A* through *F* pile was Louise Fitzhugh's classic, and she picked it up. But its pages would not flutter; its covers were firmly closed. *Shelve it. I have to shelve it first,* thought Hannah. She approached the hanging giant shelf and started placing Jordan's books in order.

When she had reached the end, with *F,* and filled one huge, long shelf, she gazed for one minute at the satisfying row of books and then reached up to take back *Harriet the Spy* for a moment. The book came off the shelf reluctantly, and Hannah sucked in her breath. There on the other side of the shelf was her own face: Hannah, at thirteen and a half, searching for a book about girls who might love girls.

For an instant, Hannah looked at Hannah. Both sets of eyes widened in stunned recognition. Then the volume of *Harriet the Spy* went *puff!,* and expelled a sheet of paper, and the book pulled itself back onto the shelf, sealing up the view into the past. Young

Hannah's face disappeared, and middle-aged Hannah was left holding a letter that seemed to have been written for young readers—those from the past, those yet to come. It was a letter, she realized, penned long ago by Jordan.

Dear young ones of the global past and future, and dear older women daring to come out at any age:

I am leaving you these books from my own time, a time when women like us had access to stories about us. I am leaving you these books because I no longer need them, but what they did for me, in giving me such comfort, I hope they'll do for you. By the time you read this I will be somewhere else, all grown up and moved on. Just know that I was like you, despite our differences.

Did you ever think you might be the only one like you? And if that special quality was hated, not only by society but in your very home, how hard did you pretend you were not you? How deeply did you hide, or lie, pretend, deny? I knew that bitter cup for years, although raised to be honest, to speak truth.

I was told that just one book could save me, but that book called me lost. Then I heard my family speak of banning other books, and so I wondered if they might hold answers. It took me years of hiding, lying, sneaking, trying, stealing, dealing, seeking, peeking, until I had the space to look for others just like me. I found them first in books.

Books! Long before we had an Internet for info by computer, I came out in a golden time of publishing, a golden era that may not be remarked on by others but was part of a great movement. I found that there were women who put the necessary readings in each other's hands and hearts.

What I want you to know is that we had a golden era of lesbian literature—publishing, presses, readings, women's studies classes, writing conferences, bookstore newsletters, even a Women's Review of Books. We discovered anew the works by women like us whose words had been suppressed, and made those titles known. We had editors and scholars, and a network of librarians who dared to put these books in young girls' hands. We determined how we would be understood, controlling the production of our memoirs and our politics.

You might have found your comfort in a bar. You didn't have to, though the bars were great and vanishing. You could walk in many cities to a bookstore, and walk into a space where some woman in tie-dye or a blue work shirt greeted you: "Hi, sister." You could go to any shelf and find your life there: Black women, Jewish women, Mormon lesbians too. You could walk out with a paperback that showed you how to love. Or even buy a blank book with encouraging quotes by women and start to write your own life by yourself.

I was in a daze for years. I walked to every bookshop selling books by lesbians. I listened to the authors who had moved me read their work. I stood behind a pillar once, too shy and overcome to say hello to Adrienne Rich, to Audre Lorde. I finally raised my head to see around me other hidden, frightened women emerging just like me, and in due time I met someone I felt that I could be with all my life. But even if you don't, you're still a thinking lesbian. I read through all the nights I didn't have a partner, and now I read to her.

These books will take you to the magic circle where we stand as witnesses to our own lives. And if these books are banned again? If all this lesbian heritage is banished, and our identity reduced again to ashes like Sappho's fragments, like Magnus Hirschfeld's library? Even if all that might remain is one rusted pin declaring DYKE, lying propped on velvet in some history museum, you will know we tried to share what we had. We may soon all be lesbians under glass. The old safe places I found are indeed vanishing: bars, bookshops, women's music festivals. That culture seems to be somehow unspeakable, as if standing in a woman-only space as an authority on your own dyke life means indifference to other lives. So does knowledge of the self disappear, and life once more becomes a ride with blacked-out windows. But I've saved, for you, this published women's knowledge. And you must write your own.

Just remember these names. Call them in your dreamtime. Not the names of authors, though you should know those too. The names of women's bookstores, where the banned books were shelved; the era of those spaces, 1971–2017; call them up as monuments to us. Amazon Books. Women and Children First. New Words. Crone's Harvest. Old Wives' Tales. Common Woman. Smedley's. Lammas.

Womanbooks. A Woman's Place. Little Sister's. Toronto Women's Bookstore. BookWoman. Streelekha Feminist Book Place. A Woman's Prerogative. Artemys. Wild Iris. Charis. Room of One's Own. Xantippe. People Called Women. Herland. Labyris. Bluestockings.

Hannah felt shock spread over her breastbone. Was this why Jordan had left city life to retire "off the grid" in some remote cabin? Did she anticipate this backlash against lesbian culture coming again so soon, just around the corner? Had she thrown up her hands in despair as one women's bookshop after another shuttered its doors?

"No time for that. Here come the patrons," said the security guard, opening again the door Hannah had come through, and suddenly she could see over the guard's tall shoulder the first eager face in a huge line of girls and women of every age from eight to eighty-eight. In an instant they had pushed through the door and were swarming toward the shelves, each floating, like the security guard, like the banned authors of the reception, ever so slightly above the floor.

Now Hannah saw again the figures from the way station Isabel had shown her, back at Halloween, girls from many nations reading forbidden literature at some safe place the Overhead patrolled; girls in head scarves, in Amish bonnets, in Hasidic school skirts, in the novice-wear that would become a nun's habit; girls who took books off the hanging shelf only to have the title instantly wriggle snakelike into the alphabet of their own language and, in some cases, an author and title of their own culture, meant only for them. Sighs of "Oh!" and "Ah!" perfumed the room with sweet breath of discovery, of homecoming, of recognition, pride. Then, each girl and woman having found the perfect book for her own coming into lesbian awakening, they sat cross-legged, chin on fist, and all around Hannah were the floating yogic bodies of girls reading, women reading, hanging *seated in the air.*

There was one girl left, standing in the doorway: the little girl turned away from the white-only library in 1959.

The security guard picked her up in her own arms, and lifted her up to the highest shelf, and seated her upon that shelf, amid the collected works of Lorraine Hansberry and Audre Lorde.

Now the room grew warm with other visitors: many of the banned authors Hannah had seen at the Reception, plus certain radical librarians of the past. She thought she saw Rose Valland, who had hidden works of art from Nazi thieves, and coded stolen pieces.

The books that Jordan had left to the Library of Congress, which Hannah had rescued, now filled just one part of the ever-increasing and expanding grand bookshelf reaching upward to a topless height. Up, up against the night sky at the end of her vision Hannah spotted Amelia Earhart's orbiting aeroplane, trailing a banner that said READ, and even beyond that she saw the white hair of the Overhead Herself sweeping books off Her desk with a huge arm, the books falling out of the sky into the outstretched hands of every young lesbian past and future. *This is the book for you. This is what you were looking for. Silence, please; we're reading.* An unusually large book flew down and bounced past Hannah's left shoulder to land gently on a special shelf: love poetry translated into Braille and raised type. Out of nowhere, the writer Karla Jay appeared with her dog Duchess and purred to

Hannah, "There's never enough erotica or history in Braille. When are you going to get busy and record it, darling?"

Books falling from the sky onto the shelf, women snuggling against one another in the air, taking notes with pens, and pencils, squealing with excitement. And the books themselves were moaning, sighing, home at last in some trusting bookworm's hands. Everyone was paging, paging, each unto each. Up, up stretched the shelves, filling and refilling without end, the contents circulating to just the right reader, across time.

How much time had elapsed in the shelving itself was unaccountable, but it was 5 a.m. Saturday morning when Hannah dragged herself, shivering, from the Library exit (opened quickly and quietly for her by the security guard, who then disappeared into an elevator that simply signaled "UP.")

The Metro wouldn't start running the weekend schedule trains for at least two hours. She walked all the way home, her empty book-bags folded flat against her sides like drained breasts. She walked home through the city, beneath which flowed the magic dust of banned books and naiads.

Her neighborhood—her gay neighborhood, her temporary home, which she'd soon be leaving (*back to what? To Isabel, to Sappho's, but no teaching job?*)— was on one of the earliest mail delivery routes in Washington, and by the time her key hit the front door-lock to her building she could see an envelope with her name on it in the lobby. The letter was from her university. Her ex-university.

She ripped apart the outer cream-smooth paper, and found this:

Please be advised that a special hearing will be convened on May 30ᵗʰ to review the upcoming conclusion of the women's history major and to appreciate the contributions made by faculty in that program. As you have long served the university as faculty in the program scheduled for retirement, we invite your participation if possible, and would welcome your testimony at this important session. RSVP.

She stood motionless, her tired mind racing, the letter heavy in her tired hand.

What if the university changed its course and saw fit to restore the women's history program? Could the faculty, alumni, and the final class of graduate students all come together at this hearing and save their program? If so, Hannah might be rehired, and even if it were just at half of her former salary, she was game. There were just as many young women who needed women's history books placed into their outstretched hands *right now* as there were girls in the past and future aching for lesbian knowledge and storylines. Hannah had given a year to time travel with rescued books; at heart, she was still a teacher. She wanted to return, so badly, to her old classroom in Building B.

(Or did the Overhead have other plans for her?)

Time to break out the academic robes, one last time.

Chapter Nine

Exhibit XX

The sense of literary purpose Hannah had felt all year now reached its end, with the Grand Reshelving a certain and completed miracle. She floated smugly through the remaining workdays of her Washington year, smiling at coworkers, occasionally bursting into nervous laughter when she passed the security guard in the halls. They never spoke. The pay phone remained quiet.

She used each lunch hour to explore Washington cafes and parks at their utter prettiest, in springtime. Her birthday came and went, with Isabel flying in as a surprise. They took a romantic Potomac River dinner cruise, saw a show at the Kennedy Center, and lost themselves in three nights of lovemaking amid the packing boxes of Hannah's rented apartment—now nearly bare again as she prepared to leave.

But what was she going back to? The near-year of sleuthing, the pay phone, the apparent assignment from the Overhead Herself had effectively suppressed all of Hannah's initial dismay and bitterness over losing her professorship.

Yet if that sacred task in Washington was now

fulfilled, Hannah faced the reality of returning to a community where she had a lover and friends and a bar community—but no job.

Late May was a blur of farewell toasts at the Library of Congress, a spending spree on souvenir paperweights from its gift ship, a bottle of brandy left at the security guard's locker, and fifteen boxes loaded into the U-Haul van that would take her back to Sappho's Bar and Grill. She no longer had her longtime apartment overlooking the university town. She moved in with Isabel for the time being, aware that "*time being*" was a broad and flexible concept in Isabel's reach, and laughing at having ticked one more item off the great lesbian list: arriving at her lover's door with a U-Haul.

Over the last weekend in May, the long Memorial Day weekend before the hearing on the 30th, Hannah studied old brochures and publicity from every women's history program in the world in order to arm herself well with rhetoric defending her own field.

The usual Memorial Day weekend campout, with all the regulars of Sappho's Bar and Grill tipsy in tents in the backwoods of one couple's cabin home, went on around her as she sat on a log, sober and focused. Letty accidentally hit a volleyball through policewoman Angie's car windshield; Moira sat down in a deep pile of skunk scat and had to borrow Trale's pants for the weekend; Carol argued with Yvette about public funding for the arts; Dog ate mushrooms and wandered around muttering. Hannah never moved from her place by the campfire.

Just once, as the embers crackled in a peculiar way, did she look up intently, thinking that she saw something in that fire. There was some historical fact she was supposed to recognize, something she had missed, in preparing for her meeting with the Dean. Something to do with fire.

❦ ❦ ❦

She woke up on the day of the hearing in Isabel's arms. "My scholar," Isabel murmured into her hair. The apartment—Isabel's apartment, *their* apartment now—smelled magnificently of buttered crumpets, Irish soda bread, rye bagels and *naan*. Not to mention sex.

Hannah yawned. "But why so much bread? Not that I don't appreciate it." She looked hungrily at the steaming breakfast tray Isabel had prepared.

Isabel played with Hannah's ears as she quoted Judy Grahn. "Because, darling—'the common woman is as common as a common loaf of bread/And will rise.'"

"Ah, quoting Judy Grahn? Guess I'd better get up then and do this," sighed Hannah, and reached for a crumpet. But Isabel said, "No, let's eat first," and pushed away the tray; then Hannah saw what she had in mind, and fell back into bed.

Hannah's board hearing was scheduled for a peculiarly specific time—1:15 p.m., putting her in mind of *The Prime of Miss Jean Brodie:* "She seeks to intimidate me by use of quarter hours."

Isabel, who had not been invited to the hearing, had promised a party in Hannah's honor to be held at Sappho's later that afternoon, optimally welcoming Hannah back to her old job if the hearing went (as they all hoped) in that direction. At noon, Isabel departed for the bar to begin the decorations and cooking prep while Hannah, feeling very alone, drove up to the university where she had so recently been a professor of women's history.

She wore her academic robes, and there was something real, important, even magical about wearing that regalia now. A fierceness of earned respect, a link to

173

the other scholarly women of the past denied a platform. She adjusted her doctoral beret ever more jauntily on her head, then briskly rubbed her hands together to be certain no traces of Isabel lingered between her fingers.

The hearing was in the Faculty Council room, an imposing space that would make even a Nobel-winning research professor feel cowed and delinquent. Severe folding chairs were set on a slight riser for the deans, and Hannah saw that past women's history faculty and some of her own recent graduate students filled rows of seats arranged at a distance from the front of the room.

The gender division was starkly apparent. All but one of the deans were male and all but one of the women's history advocates were female, but mingling in the audience were prominent alumni and donors of both sexes.

The Dean of Deans cleared his throat. "Thank you for being so prompt and responsive," he rumbled. "We recognize that the prospect of eliminating Women's History as a major has raised concerns in the larger community..."

"Concerns! How about righteous rage and offense?" shouted Dez, Hannah's star PhD candidate, who had shown up for the hearing dressed in a severe dark suit as if attending a funeral service.

"Order." The lone female dean stared at Dez. "These proceedings are intended to reassure, not to provoke, but you must *let* us proceed." Dez sat back down, cowlick spiking defiantly.

The Dean of Deans pulled a sheet of notes from a leather-topped folder. "As I'm sure you're all aware, the university has been forced to make budget cuts in order to keep with the pace of these difficult times in academia, and the humanities certainly took their

174

share. We can all agree that Professor Stern, for instance, left a bold legacy here that her students continue to appreciate, and thanks to the convenience of distance learning via Internet, she has been able to evaluate the doctoral exams of her remaining candidates. This alone demonstrates that our brick-and-mortar programs are less and less necessary, when so much learning can be shifted to online curricula."

An older woman Hannah recognized from the Board of Trustees raised her hand—a hand without any wedding band, Hannah noted. "Dean, of course we all recognize the benefits and necessary innovations of the digital age. But isn't there something to be said for traditional classroom instruction? For instance, aren't many female students actually drawn to the women's history program because of, well, that ambience of sisterhood that may well be lacking in other required on-campus classes?"

Another dean shook his head. "We can no longer in good faith be partial to one gender in our outreach. Too many concerned students and alumni have questioned the legality of offering women's studies when we don't offer men's studies as well . . ."

A collective groan went up. "Really, how clueless is this administration?" complained Hannah's old colleague from the Art department. "Women's history became an option precisely because every other humanities class preaches men's history. I still get blowback for introducing *three* female artists amid the tiresome canon of famous men. Are you advocating a White Studies curriculum to balance out the Black Studies major we finally, finally instituted?"

"Of course not," thundered the Dean. "But we found that a satellite faculty of just three tenured professors could teach all accredited courses in History that touch on women of the past, thus eliminating the need for courses in a separately funded women's history concentrate."

Hannah looked with horror at these three select faculty from the university who would now be covering anything to do with women. One was a devout Baptist who believed women belonged in the home, another was a contemporary gender theorist who taught that there was no such thing as a woman, and the third was notorious for being drunk during his office hours and fondling his graduate assistants.

Hannah raised her hand to speak, and the Dean of Deans shook his head. "Please wait. We also know that for many of our students *women's studies* and *women's history* are no longer relevant categories in scholarship that takes a nonbinary perspective. Thus we are also giving our past graduates the opportunity to redact their diplomas and change their women's history degrees to History of Gender, on request."

He looked around in expectation of approval for this recent innovation. But a palpable current of dissent flickered through the room as both conservative alumni and radical feminist grad students took in this official banishment of the category *Woman*.

Disappearance.

Erasure.

Hannah stood up, flicking her robes away from the sad faces of her graduate students.

"Look, as an historian, I wish to offer some historical perspective here," she began, feeling her heart rate increase with every word. "We not only had—*have*—one of the best women's history programs in the state, we have majors in women's studies too, and an international women's leadership institute, and a women's issues-themed house dorm! In every one of these you have dynamic students doing research on women. Are you going to eradicate all of these as outmoded, too

176

costly, unnecessary? Are you intending to remove the word *woman* from every program simultaneously? What message does that send to the female students? They make up over 55 percent of the student body."

One whiskered gentleman rose from the back of the room, nodded at Hannah, and raised his palm to speak. "As one of this university's more generous donors, I must say I'm appalled by what I've just heard," he began. "This young lady is a prime example of how this university wastes its resources. It's eye-opening to be here today."

Then he added, "Truly? Am I hearing this right? We've been offering a women's studies undergraduate program *and* a women's history MA *and* some sort of feminist dorm? What an excess of ridiculousness. We can do without all of that. Our students come here to *learn*."

Hannah's face fell.

And it went downhill from there. She mustered every statistic and data spread she had prepared, proving the importance of women's history to women who had gone K-12 with no mention of their foremothers. She offered ways the university might save money without eliminating the program.

Finally, Hannah pointed out that "A well-used quote attributed to Sojourner Truth is '*Ain't I a woman?*' She didn't say '*Ain't I a fluid nonbinary category?*' On that basis alone, I'd argue for keeping the original name of our research program."

But the Dean remained adamant. Women's history was, now, history.

Then Dez and the four other PhD candidates present, all in their mid-twenties and today all dressed alike in dark suits, suddenly stood up. In one quick motion they pulled the long tablecloth away from an extra side table located behind their row of folding chairs. Reaching below the table, they brought out—could it be? A girl-sized pine-box casket, draped in the tricolors of the women's suffrage movement and partly open to reveal (thankfully) not a body, but dozens of award-winning women's history textbooks. Resting on top was Hannah's last book.

"Dearly beloved, we are gathered here today to bury the women's history program at this university," Dez recited from notes sketched on her sweaty palm as the four pallbearers lifted the box to shoulder height and began a death march around the perimeter of the room. "We mark the end of an era with the rending of our coats." Each woman ripped the lapel of her own blazer. "And we will fast for those sisters in struggle who still hunger for this knowledge."

She pulled a slip of paper from her torn blazer. "Here are all the university women's studies and women's history programs in America that have dropped the word *woman* from their title and now are Gender Studies. Here are all the Gender Studies programs that this past year offered no courses on women, no courses on lesbians, no *L*. Here are all the students in America who will never learn how women like us survived." As she began to read aloud, necks craned, jaws dropped, the female dean called for order, and Hannah's previous Chair ran from the room, eyes downcast, head shaking.

Dez paused in front of Hannah. "We will bury this body of work underneath lecture hall B-12, your old classroom," she spoke firmly. "And then we will complete our doctorates, the last women's history doctorates from this school, on schedule but very long distance. We choose to retain *WOMAN* on our diplomas. And Dr. Stern will have her tenure in our hearts."

Hannah gasped, recognizing the phrase she

thought she herself had invented. *Very long distance.* Across time? Where were they all going?

Other heads turned as one of the two alumni board representatives walked toward the exit, calling over his shoulder, "The best news I heard here today is that we don't offer tenure to any of these radical feminists." The door slammed behind him, sending a thin burst of dust into the air.

Those dust motes seemed to dance before her eyes. Hannah blinked as they landed cruelly on her lashes, in her brows. The dust was thick, then flat, quickly taking the shape of swirling ashes. She was standing on a crossed pyre of badly sawed and broken boughs and castoff planking, and the walls of the university boardroom had opened into a public square filled with curious, pitying faces.

At her feet were leather-bound and hand-illuminated volumes of women's history; she saw that her feet were tied to a pole that pushed upward against her back, meeting the splintered crosspiece to which her hands were bound. Bewigged men approached her with torches, questioning her in Latin, a language she barely recognized as it spread between their parted, decayed teeth.

The upward swirling ashes were the writings of her ancestors, her foremothers, her teachers; their hot ink made the air smell bitter. The ash-dust filled her eyes; her tears rolled down, but not enough in number to put out the spreading flames. She vaguely glimpsed the man who had slammed out the door, delighted to be rid of women's history. He pointed to her smoky burning legs and said, *she'll lose that leg hair now.* And even as her own erasure started, she thought at once of Oscar Wilde on trial, sentenced to hard labor. And a woman, yes, a woman had sneered at the gay man and declared, *he'll have his hair cut reg'lar now!*

Suddenly an ember danced before her eyes, the ember that had seemed to speak to her from the fire at the Memorial Day campout (*wasn't that just two days ago?*) This was what she had failed to recognize, *failed*, yes, as a historian, to remember. It was the 30th of May. She was on trial with women's history on the anniversary of Joan of Arc's burning.

And now Hannah was burning. She was burning along with all the canceled lectures on women's history, lesbian culture, feminism. She was Hirschfeld's library, she was Joan of Arc, she was a witch possessed by women's history. How could she think they would let her live, let alone continue with her very dangerous work?

But where was the Overhead? Wouldn't she intervene now and rescue Hannah? But then why had she not intervened and rescued Joan? Or (*don't go there, don't go there*) if there was in fact any such powerful Goddess, why had any of history's tragedies occurred? The witch burnings. Famine and plague. Slavery. Genocide. Woman-hating, homophobia, racism, poverty. The Holocaust . . .

And when the flames dared to reach her writing hand, she wrenched forth the desperate last thought: *This is why they call it being "fired."*

With her last energy Hannah turned her head to the left and saw, standing at the edge of the jeering crowd, Isabel in a nun's habit, hands clasped under her robe.

Isabel. Maybe this is just one of her time travel schemes! Not funny. Not sexy. It hurts! Isabel! Did you cast a spell and make me Joan of Arc?

And Isabel shook her head and seemed to speak without moving her lips. What she told Hannah now was *You were always Joan of Arc. The spell of ages turned you into Dr. Hannah Stern. You were truly Joan, and*

Hypatia, and Anne Hutchinson and all those burned for their daring. Out of their ashes I brewed you into Hannah for our time.

"Ow!" Hannah snapped back to the council room and saw that she had inadvertently put her outstretched hand onto the hot coffee urn, its blazing fire ring still turned high. Her palm was already beginning to blister. "Let's get you out of here," whispered Cassandra, her favorite faculty colleague through their many teaching years, and Hannah half-walked, half-trotted out the door with a lemonade-soaked napkin wrapped around her right hand, leaving a phalanx of funeral-dressed grad students in loud argument with the Dean.

Later, at Sappho's Bar and Grill, they raised sad glasses to the ruined afternoon. Without a women's history program at the university, not just Hannah but all the other women faculty in affiliated positions were about to lose their jobs and move away, taking with them the students, graduate students, librarians, and all the annually returning and regenerating bodies that had been the bar community for decades, ever since the women's history program had started in the late 1970s.

What is the price of a feminist community? How do you reckon its loss, its downgrading to dispensable? No beer could numb that pain—though Isabel, as ever, was busily mixing herbs to bring them through.

"You were right to take that Library of Congress gig," Letty told Hannah, one calloused hand slapping her on the backside. "Not much left for you up on that campus. Maybe we all ought to get down to the business of preserving our books 'n' papers. You're practically the only one I can trust with my high school diary; and what about Trale over there? She's got years up on *me*. Trale, you *are* dyke history. Where you gonna leave your papers? Get Hannah to put 'em in order, and fast. We can't even count on women's studies to keep our stories passed along the line!"

"No. Stay here in town and fight. I'm not ready to be a museum piece," Moira argued. "Putting our community into an archive—that feels like giving in. Preserving the mere idea of us when we're still alive, when the bar is doing fine. Isn't it?" She looked at Isabel, then burst into tears.

Isabel moved quickly to stand in the circle of angry, confused bar patrons. "This community is safe," she assured Moira, and Letty, and Dog and Yvette and Trale. "I'm keeping the bar going as long as you need. But we can't hide from the changes of history, of our own time. This is one of the last women's bars to have a private membership and café. We might well have a memorial in the manner Hannah's grad students staged today, reciting instead the names of former lesbian bars."

"We created a time capsule right from the beginning," Trale nodded. "Before the bar even opened so those who came later would be sure to see us for who we were. Not just a random collection of characters, but a tribe. A family. That capsule should be updated right now, this afternoon, while we're all here." She stood up, knees creaking. "Anyone with me?"

"Well, if I could pick any dyke bar to be *the* dyke bar for display, it would be us here in this fuckin' awesome space," Letty went on, ignoring the fresh panic on Moira's face. "I mean, we are *it*. Maybe we've always been kinda museum-ready, not because we're aging out but because we're still major full-on. You want a showcase bar some future kids can learn from, you won't do better than what we had here. I mean, what we still have here," she corrected herself; but it was too late.

Too late.

Hannah saw it. They all saw it: Isabel's lips moving to shape the four words they recognized, on a regular basis, as the start to anything odd happening. Isabel was murmuring, "*So mote it be.*"

"*No!*" shouted Hannah.

Then Isabel seemed to spill outward, colorfully, like a poured dosage of strong paint spreading to fill a palette, and her voice boomed out an unexpected question—yet recognizable as a question every one of them had carried in their hearts all year: "*Would you rather fade out over the coming years, ever less powerful, or disappear at your peak, forever remembered at your Amazon best?*"

And, with a puff of lavender smoke, the bar vanished. The doors slammed shut on a platform of wood and walls that glowed, just briefly, and then faded into air.

Hannah felt herself plunged into a whirlwind of paper and heat, bodies and moisture, spilled beer and song sheets. She grabbed for Isabel's hand. Isabel's hand slipped from hers. There was only Isabel's voice calling, "Wait for me there," and then a swift lateral plunge into warm darkness. Falling, but not falling. A sense of *placement* by an unseen hand, or hands.

Then lights came on again, most peculiarly as though streaming from the disco ball of the bar—the mechanism inside of which Trale and other founding members had once hidden the 1970s time capsule of the old bar. The disco ball was turning, and Hannah felt herself dancing—her feet not quite on the floor.

She was dancing, but bumping up against a sharp edge like a wall, a defined space at the side of the floor. Something smooth and hard surrounded her at arms' length. *Glass!*

"I had to do it," thundered a voice, and she looked up to see the Overhead Herself, projecting the sorrowful wise light of her ancient eyes downward through the bar's disco ball; and Hannah saw that other mortal heads were also downward-peering as the Overhead faded back. The top of the bar had become a closed but see-through wall, filled with staring faces. The entire bar had been transported, all of them, except Isabel (*where are you, Isabel?*)—transported in perfect miniaturized preservation to the long glass case of the Great Hall in the Library of Congress.

They were inside the first-ever exhibit on lesbian bars. No: they *were* the exhibit. Their bar was on display, and they were sealed in it, with no visible way out for any of the membership.

They had become—all of them—lesbians under glass.

Everyone stood stock still, looking upward. Enormous tourists gawked at the tiny lesbians, some laughing and pointing, some taking photographs with exotic mobile devices Hannah had never seen before. *We must be in the future, a not-too-distant future,* she thought, straining to see if any of the bodies above them were clothed in sweatshirts with telltale NCAA tournament dates or graduation years. Her own watch had stopped again.

There! There was Isabel, back behind the bar, mixing drinks as if nothing unusual had occurred.

She had managed to stay cool and collected even in miniature, even with her bar served up as a remnant of late twentieth-/early twenty-first century dyke life. "Calm down," she ordered. "Look around. The bar is preserved here in its entirety. Can you not understand?"

Panicked cries subsided to puzzled silence. Then Letty announced, "Hell, yeah. Everything came with us. Bar still functions, right? Pool balls move? So we get to party on. I'll have a beer—or eight. Trale, get over here and chalk that cue up. Damn if it ain't playtime for all eternity!"

"Not all eternity," Isabel suggested. "Just a rehearsal. Moira, you said you weren't ready to be a museum piece yet. But someone has to want us enough to keep us going in our own time. Our inheritors will have to bring us back, so we can live out our real lives in full."

As she spoke, more enormous heads loomed over them, this time four cultural anthropologists taking notes. Shoni gave them the finger, yelling, "Not again! First my ancestors, then me? Get me out of this museum!"

Why couldn't the Overhead intervene? Why had the Overhead put them there? Was this the next assignment? But couldn't the Overhead prevent the vanishing of lesbian culture—keep it going just a little bit longer in Hannah's time?

Then Hannah recalled her long-ago first meeting with the Overhead, a Goddess in exile whose desk was littered with the material culture of women's history. She would express her frustration by occasionally sweeping one long arm across her desk to scatter goddess figures and papers and gems off the desk's edge, letting artifacts land in earthly fissures, caves, and cracks. Patriarchy had reduced the reach of Her power. Like Hannah, She had been denied tenure. All She was able to do was scatter women's heritage where it might be rediscovered and appraised in a future time. A powerful rain: of memories from Her powerful reign.

Hannah's generation of women's history scholars had carefully examined those ancient goddess sculptures and carvings and cuneiform writings to understand lost rituals women once celebrated. So why wouldn't Hannah's own tribe of party-throwing dykes be of interest to future historians? Would these later scholars be able to understand, by observing a model lesbian bar, how lesbians like Hannah had lived? Would they piece together broken shards of Olivia records and hear the siren songs of Cris Williamson?

And in the future maybe everything was preserved, yet moving, under glass. Jordan Matthews had warned of this! In her letter to future readers! She had scrawled fiercely, "*Even if all that might remain is one rusted pin declaring DYKE lying propped on velvet in some history museum, you will know we tried to share what we had. We may soon all be lesbians under glass . . .*" It was already happening, anyway, thought Hannah. Her own undergraduate students had preferred to read on glass. Their encounters with women's writing came from a tablet, a computer, a laptop.

But at Sappho's Bar and Grill, there was another aspect. They were all under glass because they were under the spell of Isabel's drinks. Isabel had crossed time and space to collect and bottle the essence of lesbians and serve it back to the community, Sappho's fragments soaking in oceans and rivers of time, water drawn up by women and girls who spread that lost poetry over their fields and gardens, food grown and fed to other women who birthed daughters nursed with breast milk formed from poet-water's nutrients.

Isabel had the essence of lesbians stored in the bar's wine cellar, *bottled* in the cellar, enough original essence to re-create all the lesbian energy of time. That had been Isabel's assignment, to be the great Mixologist and Brewmistress who took the best women in any community, introduced them, and mixed their hearts with essences of others. In the veins of each member of Sappho's Bar, lesbian history flowed. And if the bar was preserved in its entirety under glass, that meant the wine cellar had to be accessible, too, for these anthropologists of the future to pass along, preserve.

Or maybe no one in the future cared at all. What if *future* administrators at the Library saw this very queer exhibit as just a temporary attraction, then shoved it in a box for remote storage?

They could be suffocated in some archival packing crate, like the one Hannah had rescued from off-site agony—never seen, handled, touched, loved, known, ever again. They'd have to wait for some future Hannah Stern person to reshelve them, get them back to their own time. And if nobody cared?

Her panicked existentialism was interrupted by Yvette's practical action. "Hey!" Yvette shouted. "We all still have our cell phones. Let's call our families!"

Hands reached into back pockets, coat pockets, backpacks. There was a moment of mad scramble. Then:

"I can't get a signal," Carol wailed.

"I can't get on Wi-Fi," Dog howled.

But Hannah stood up from her favorite padded barstool, and walked unsteadily toward the bar's old wall phone, dangling as ever in its built-in shelf. She caught her lover's eye, and Isabel nodded. Then Hannah dialed 202-554-4876.

Deep within the Library of Congress, a very old pay phone began to ring in the visitors' ladies' room.

It rang and rang, and they all waited, the good women of Sappho's Bar and Grill. Who would answer the call? Who would rescue lesbian life and culture from being stifled under glass, relegated to history, made into a museum piece before its time? Who would revive the old-fashioned dyke bar, rebuild women's bookstores, produce women's music festivals again?

The next generation. The next generation. The next generation.

"But they have to want to," Trale put in. "They have to want us." She looked at Isabel and at Hannah, both of whom were forty years younger than herself. "You wanted me around. You kept it up: this bar, dyke herstory. So, it's possible that the next round will keep a place for you, like you kept a place for me. Hell, we all have more than one life. Wasn't Joan of Arc made a saint, eventually?" She went back to shooting pool.

Ring. Ring.

Moira wept openly, Yvette clenching her hand. Shoni lit sage. Bits of smoke escaped from the chipped edges of the glass case, startling the visitors above.

The visitors above . . .

"Look!" Hannah pointed. There, in the Great North Hall, in one painted mural on the ceiling far above the display case imprisoning them, was the only image of a woman among the many murals of famous men. How had she forgotten? She'd walked under this mural every day during her year of work at the Library of Congress, smiling to herself.

"It's a mural of Sappho," Dog said, awed.

"It's the portal to the Overhead," said Hannah. "Sappho is the Overhead Projector, and the Overhead's Protector."

"I sure as shit don't know what-all *that* means," Letty complained.

Ring. Hannah knew they needed someone. She had always been married to the movement and now she needed someone else to want, that badly, to be wedded to lesbian culture. Someone to step up to their altar and vow to protect them, through sickness and health. *Ring.* "And with this ring I do thee wed . . ." *Ring.* O, younger generation, will you marry us?

And in the bathroom, someone picked up the phone. Hannah heard the unmistakable low voice of her graduate student, Dez, tentatively saying, "Hello?"

That's right! She promised to come to Washington after finishing her dissertation. She promised to work with me Very Long Distance. She must have headed to D.C. and the Library of Congress right after burying those textbooks at my old classroom. Why that classroom? Hannah wondered suddenly, though recognizing it as the last place she'd ever stood at a lectern and taught.

But she already knew the answer. Dez had taken the old, unused, overhead projector that had started Hannah's journey one year back. Dez, twenty years younger than Hannah, was the next generation that stood by to inherit her community's power, to continue working in women's history, with Sappho as her guide. Dez, faithful to them here in a future decade, could open that portal above them, and project them back to their own time, where the younger Dez needed Hannah and the bar members to mentor her forward. They'd fly back under Sappho's wings, Amelia Earhart guiding them, the bar and its essences returned safely and good for one more generation—and maybe more.

Isabel stood by nodding as Hannah clutched the phone.

"Hello?" said Dez, the pilot of the next generation, ready to fly very long distance in service to women's history. And Hannah whispered, "Save us. Save us. Save us."

Acknowledgments

This is a work of fiction, with certain liberties taken regarding the Library of Congress "loading dock" and other aspects. However, there is indeed a mural of Sappho on the ceiling of the Jefferson Building, and a pay phone in the women's bathroom on the first floor, with the phone number 202-554-4876. For immersion in the culture and structure of the Library of Congress, I am grateful to librarian Meg Metcalf and my colleagues in the LOC Women's History and Gender Studies Discussion Group. For discussion on aspects of curating at the Smithsonian, I thank my friend Katherine Ott. For insights on library book culling, shredding, and repair, I thank Laura Brezel. For the time and space to work on this manuscript, I am most grateful to Veronica Calarco and my friends at the Stiwdio Maelor residency in Corris, Wales. Finally, I am of course grateful for the thoughtful guidance and enthusiastic support I enjoy at Bywater Books.

About the Author

Bonnie Morris earned her PhD in women's history from Binghamton University and has taught Sports and Gender for over twenty years at campuses ranging from UC Berkeley to Georgetown and George Washington Universities. She is the author of sixteen books, including three Lambda Literary Finalists (*Eden Built by Eves, Girl Reel, Revenge of the Women's Studies Professor*), two national first-prize chapbooks (*The Schoolgirl's Atlas, Sixes and Sevens*) and the critical feminist texts *Women's History for Beginners, The Feminist Revolution*, and *The Disappearing L.* Her recent exhibit on women's music at the Library of Congress broke new ground in showcasing lesbian albums, and she is now a historical consultant to the Smithsonian Institute, the AP U.S. History exam, Disney Animation, the State Department's International Visitor program and the Global Women's Institute. She may be found lecturing on C-Span, Olivia Cruises, Semester at Sea, the National Women's Music Festival, and on Pacifica Radio KPFK.

SAPPHO'S
BAR AND GRILL

"Holy Hildegarde of Bingen! Bonnie Morris brings history to vivid, hilarious life in this whip-smart time travel tour de force." —ALISON BECHDEL, Author of *Fun Home*

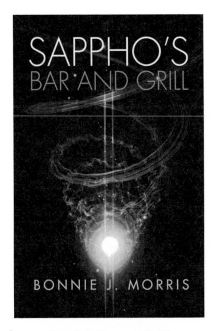

Sappho's Bar and Grill
by Bonnie J. Morris
Print 978-1-61294-097-7
Ebook 978-1-61294-098-4

www.bywaterbooks.com

Bywater
BOOKS

At Bywater Books we love good books about lesbians just like you do, and we're committed to bringing the best of contemporary lesbian writing to our avid readers. Our editorial team is dedicated to finding and developing outstanding writers who create books you won't want to put down.

We sponsor the Bywater Prize for Fiction to help with this quest. Each prizewinner receives $1,000 and publication of their novel. We have already discovered amazing writers like Jill Malone, Sally Bellerose, and Hilary Sloin through the Bywater Prize. Which exciting new writer will we find next?

For more information about Bywater Books and the annual Bywater Prize for Fiction, please visit our website.

www.bywaterbooks.com